S0-BDJ-838

The
Silhouette Maker
of
Copenhagen

The Judge's Chambers

The Judge's Chambers and Other Stories

The Lawyer's Chambers and Other Stories

The Last Jewish Shortstop in America

The Night Swimmer—A Man in London and Other
Stories

Conversations with a Golden Ballerina

The Humpback of Lodz

The Legal Fiction of Lowell B. Komie

The
Silhouette Maker
of
Copenhagen

A Novella & Stories

Lowell B. Komie

Swordfish/Chicago
Publishers

Copyright © 2006 by Lowell B. Komie. All rights reserved. Printed in the
United States of America. No part of this book may be used or repro-
duced in any manner whatsoever without written permission except in the
case of brief quotations embodied in critical articles and reviews. For information, address Swordfish/Chicago, Publishers, 431Elm Street, Deer-
field, Illinois 60015.

Book design: Miles Zimmerman
Book production: The Chestnut House Group, Inc.

Library of Congress Control Number: 2005910067

Komie, Lowell B.

   The Silhouette Maker of Copenhagen

   1. Fiction   I. Title

ISBN: 0-9641957-6-3

"A Woman in Prague" and "A Woman in Warsaw" were published in *The
Chicago Tribune Magazine,* "Lederhosen Boys" in *The Milwaukee Journal
Magazine,* and "A Commuter's Notes", Chapter 1, in *The CBA Record,* the
magazine of the Chicago Bar Association.

For my friend Lon Romanski

Contents

Preface

IT IS MY INTENTION WITH THIS COLLECTION to continue my efforts to write about the Holocaust. That is the single thread that connects all these stories. The "Silhouette Maker of Copenhagen" as a novella takes place in Copenhagen and touches upon the courage of the Danish people in saving their Jewish citizens in the face of the German occupation. The novella is not centered on the Holocaust but has a humorous core as its major theme, and in that context it is difficult for a writer to even touch upon events of the Holocaust.

The other stories have no humor at all. "A Commuter's Notes" tells the story of a man on a train. It's a daily diary of his thoughts, including his memory of his family who came to America from Lithuania and other members of the family who stayed behind and have never been heard from again. He dreams of returning to Lithuania to find their killers. "A Woman in Warsaw" and "A Woman in Prague" were published by *The Chicago Tri-*

bune Magazine to an audience of over 3 million people. They both deal with the Holocaust and arise from my experiences in Eastern Europe when I was assigned by *Chicago Magazine* to go to Warsaw in 1984. For that assignment I will always be grateful to my dear friend John Fink who was then the editor of *Chicago Magazine*. The story "Lederhosen Boys" was published in *The Milwaukee Journal Magazine* and arose from my memories of the German-American Bund when I was a boy in the late 1930s growing up in Milwaukee. The final story of the collection, *Messenger*, has never been published. It tells the story of a high school boy who takes it upon himself to work as a Western Union delivery boy during World War II and becomes the death messenger of the town.

I write about the Holocaust because I want to honor the six million Jews who died and whose voices have been forever silenced. While I am alive and have the ability to carry on as a writer I want to speak for them. Many of them would have been wonderful poets, writers, and artists had they been allowed to live. Their voices have been silenced forever. I hope that these stories will serve their memory.

The
Silhouette Maker
of
Copenhagen

L·B·K

1

HIS NAME IS JONNY LEVIN. He has come to Copenhagen on his sabbatical, perhaps to write a history. What kind of history? He doesn't really know. He's always wanted to write a history of the Levin family, but has never attempted it. He's an English professor at one of the Universities in Chicago. Let's leave it nameless. All we can say is that it has a football team. Last term he taught a new course on Jewish Literature. It was a first for the university and he established it. It was the last course he taught before leaving for his sabbatical year. He's 62 and twice divorced with two daughters from his fractious first marriage. He lives alone in a large two-bedroom flat in Evanston in an old 1920s courtyard brown brick building with two regal lions on colonnades with cannonballs in their paws guarding its entrance.

He and his second wife, Ramona, had lived there for ten years until their divorce. They had no children. The second divorce was friendly. They just split and went their separate ways—

she to California and he to his sabbatical year. It's April, 2005. He'd always wanted to visit Denmark. He felt drawn to this small, courageous country because of its rescue of its Jewish citizens during the war. He knew he would feel comfortable among the Danes. Just being among them would be a comfort to him and he wouldn't feel so alone. Also, instead of a history of the Levin family, he really wanted to attempt to write a novel. He had a quiet flame insisting that if only he would try, he would be successful. He would perhaps be likened to an undiscovered Bellow. He could be an undiscovered and even more misunderstood Roth. Or perhaps Irwin Shaw, no, no longer Irwin Shaw, Shaw's dead. Perhaps Bernard Malamud, no, also dead, Alfred Kazin, dead. Lionel Trilling, dead. But Jonny Levin, a talented unknown Jewish novelist with a bizarre and whimsical sense of humor, still alive with this tiny secret flame burning of a novelist *manqué*. But since the divorce, blocked. He hasn't been able to write a word.

Actually, the name is Professor John Levin, not Jonny Levin. Perhaps this is the beginning of whimsy? Jonny Levin is only a pseudonym he's been using the four days he's been in Denmark. It makes him feel slightly Danish and allows him to blend and not be just an aging, dried out American professor on sabbatical, but seemingly a youthful energetic Jewish Dane. A Dane still with some liveliness in his heart and vigor and longing. So, a Dane simply named, the name foreshortened, John to Jon and given the diminutive Jonny. Is this the beginning of a farce? No, it's just the changing of a name.

He's staying at the Hotel Angleterre, a small hotel right on the edge of Copenhagen's red light district. The hotel has a dignified paneled lobby with leather, brass-studded chairs and two gracious, even beautiful, blonde Danish women in their mid-twenties behind the front desk, dressed in black waist-coats and bow ties, politely greeting him each evening and handing him his key on a large, oblong wooden block. He doesn't know the Danish word for key, but he does know the word for thank you, *Tak*, and he says thank you to them. *Tak*. They smile at an American who tries to speak Danish and answer him with the same word, *Tak*. So he converts it to "*Tak, Tak* Jonny Levin" as the answer that spins through his mind, the two lovely blondes still whirring in his head as the elevator doors close and it begins its ascent. "*Tak, Tak,* Jonny Levin." Each of the four nights he's been here he's hesitated at the front door of his hotel before going up to his room to look down the street Colbjornsengade to see if there were any prostitutes on the street, but so far he's seen no one. He feels like a rather foolish man gazing down the street each night for prostitutes, but he's far from foolish. He simply wants to learn the rhythm of the city, and more importantly the rhythm of himself in this city.

So far each night he's had dinner outdoors in a restaurant in Tivoli, the beautiful gardens and amusement park. It's early in April and the restaurants are chilly but open. He's only spoken to two people at Tivoli. One is the young woman in charge of a shooting booth where you can target shoot at clay targets with a compressed air pellet rifle. She's perhaps 18. The other woman is a woman almost his age, in her late fifties. She's a tall, heavy woman with a seamed face in charge of a roulette wheel in the section of Tivoli devoted to slot machines and roulette. She says "Skål" perfunctorily to him when he wins. She's like a peasant lady croupier. It's not really a roulette wheel. It's more like an old-fashioned wooden carnival wheel and you bet one kroner pieces on symbols, caricatures, farm animal figures, numbers and flags. He's picked the American flag as his symbol and each night has come back to the hotel with a small plastic sack half full of kroner pieces. His winnings. They're only worth a dime, which, at best, isn't worth anything in Denmark. It's just half of a small plastic sack full of dimes. Perhaps a total of five or six dollars.

After dinner tonight, the fourth night, he again headed toward the shooting booth down the flower-edged gravel paths of Tivoli. He'd had a good meal, again outdoors, different types of small boiled potatoes, and four different types of herring. Herring and sour cream, herring and mustard sauce, herring with onions, and matjes herring, all this over thick slabs of dark Danish bread and washed down with glasses of Carlsberg beer and a tiny glass of Aquavit on the side.

The bored young woman at the shooting booth looked up and smiled at him tonight when she saw him coming down the path and handed him the same rifle he'd used last night. The prizes are foolish little things. A caricature of a Tivoli toy soldier guard standing in his striped conical guard's hut in his red waist coat and bearskin hat. A China cup with a photo of Queen Magrethe, some balloons on sticks, a red paddle with a white ball on a rubber band, the usual teddy bears and stuffed animals. Some multi-colored joss sticks, some of which have been lit, are set in a gold rimmed dish wafting incense across the front of the shooting booth. The combination of the incense and the Aquavit blurs his vision, and he holds the heavy stock of the rifle to his cheek. Last night, of ten shots, he'd put eight on the target, even two in the tiny circle of the bulls eye. The young attendant had said nothing. Neither approbation nor disapproval, but without expression she tore off his target sheet and handed it to him as he left. He'd come close. Three shots in the bulls eye circle would have won a prize. He kept the paper target and had it propped up on the dresser in his room if the maid hadn't thrown it away. Tonight the gun swayed as he aimed not at a bulls eye sheet, but at a rack of clay pipes. If he could shatter four pipes in the rack he'd win his choice of a Danish flag lapel pin or a figure of the Little

Mermaid. He aimed at the pipes and blinked several times to clear the blurring and then held his breath and squeezed off the first shot. He shattered the first pipe, hitting it exactly on the bowl. He moved the rifle to the left, just a minute adjustment, held his breath for a long moment, blinked again to clear his vision and squeezed the trigger. He shattered the bowl of the second pipe. Again, an infinitely miniscule adjustment, he held his breath, and squeezed and he hit the third pipe. Now only one more for a prize. He rested for a moment and looked over at the attendant. She was a typical red-faced Danish teenager, with a cherub face, a tiny snub nose, blonde hair held in back with a large plastic clip, and fair blue eyes. She was listening to a yellow tape deck with ear phones and dropping pellets in a tube. But tonight she was also watching him. He knew she was watching him. He aimed again, but this time he wet the front sight of the rifle with saliva on his finger. He'd seen Gary Cooper do that in a movie, "Sergeant York". He aimed and immediately smashed the fourth clay bowl.

The young woman got down off her perch and said to him, "You're a good shot," in an almost-perfect English accent. "Americans love to shoot. You're early though. We don't get them in spring, only in the summer. Do you have shooting booths like this in America? What do you want, the Little Mermaid?"

"No, the pin."

She handed him his trophy, a Danish flag lapel pin. She dropped it into his hand.

"We have shooting booths on the main boulevards in most of our cities," he told her.

"So you practiced before you came over here."

"Yes I practiced."

He thanked her and put the Danish flag lapel pin on,

pinning it on the lapel of his navy blue sports coat and with his blue jacket and his red and white lapel pin, he thought he looked like a Danish yachtsman. All he needed was a white yachtsman's cap. While he'd been shooting, a group of Spanish tourists had quietly gathered around him, standing silently watching him. "Good evening," he said to them in English as he left, and several people smiled but didn't answer him. He could hear a few words of Spanish, "Buenos Noches," he said to them and pointed to the rifles, "Buena Suerte." Was that the right phrase for good luck? One of the men, short with glasses and in a yellow sweater smiled up at him as he hugged his wife to protect her from the chill.

He walked down the flowered gravel paths of Tivoli wearing his Danish flag pin, a white cross on a red background, and went out the old wooden archway gate and crossed Hans Christian Andersen Boulevard. He'd seen the hulking bronze statue of the seated figure of Andersen across the boulevard. It was a nice touch, placing a statue of the old poet directly across from the amusement park. He crossed the street and he was alone with the huge statue of Andersen who was shown seated wearing a top hat and a cravat and a long waistcoat, holding a cane in one hand and a book in the other, his head turned up in the direction of Tivoli. What about giving a little hello to Andersen? A little shry in the moonlight with the bulb-lit towers of the Tivoli pagodas in the background. A shry for all the pain the old bachelor writer had to endure to grind out those magical tales. A Reichean shry. He'd read James Atlas's biography of Bellow. According to Atlas, Bellow practiced Reichean primal scream therapy sitting on the benches of Hyde Park in Chicago. He put his hand on Hans Christian Andersen's hand, over his thick fingers holding the book. They were worn smooth from so many tourists' hands touching them. He opened his mouth. Not a word. Not even a sound. Andersen's smooth bronze fingers were as cold as the barrel of the gun. The only sounds were the shrieks of the riders dropping from the parachute towers at Tivoli. Finally a sound came out of his own mouth and it sounded like – eech – a weak little glottal puff. Not even a shry. Not a cry. Bellow would have really sounded off in the moonlight in Copenhagen. When he was Jonny Levin's age, he would have given Andersen a real primal shry in honor of Andersen's work. Bellow fathered a daughter at 83 and wrote a novel, *Ravelstein*. And he, Jonny Levin, he Jonny Levin could only manage – "eech". But maybe, by touching Andersen's hand, he'd unblock and he'd be able to go back to the room and write something marvelous.

2

INSTEAD OF THE TWO lovely blondes on duty at the hotel desk, he was met by a sour-faced old man doing a crossword puzzle in the evening paper who said nothing to him when he handed him his key. Also no prostitutes were hanging around the hotel on the street, just some kids beered up and singing. Many of them wearing those silly little white yachting caps. He was told that those white caps signified candidates for graduation from high school so he really didn't need one to go with his blue blazer and the Danish flag pin.

Up in the room, he sat on the edge of the bed and turned on Danish TV. Some kind of quiz show with two dour tweed-jacketed men and a big breasted cheerful hostess. He watched for a moment but couldn't understand a word, and muted it. He took his writing tablet out of the night stand drawer and found a pen and wrote two lines.

KAENE MICKEY BERNSTEIN
(MARRIED TO ROSE LEVIN)

Perhaps this would be the beginning of his Levin Family history which hopefully he could turn into a novel if he could just keep the faces of his old loves from suddenly appearing. For years he'd been carrying a set of images of his old loves, college girls, high school girls, women from his bachelor days and lately they would appear flashing through his mind almost every day, particularly in the morning in the shower, or in the evenings just before he went to bed. In the evenings, the faces would always appear about this time so if he was to do any serious work he would have to stop them. *Kaene* is the Danish word for "Dear". He'd cut through a small church cemetery during his exploration today and he'd seen the word "Kaene" chiseled into the gravemarkers before the name on many headstones. The stones were small compared to American headstones. He would read "Kaene Peter Christiansen," date of birth, date of death. Or "Kaene Margaret Mortensen", date of birth, date of death. Or "Kaene Peter Jensen". The stones were also often bordered by one or two tiny songbirds modeled on the top edge of the gravemarkers, perhaps a set of lovebirds or doves or pigeons. Often "Kaene Peter Christiansen, etc." would be finished off with a separate line … *Tak*. On some stones, a separate line, *Tak Tak Tak*. Again, *Tak*, the word for thank you. So apparently you have "Dear Peter Christiansen" thanking those who have come to visit his grave. He was told by an older man dressed in formal black with a white wing bow-tie, some aide in the church, that *Kaene* is the word for "dear" and instead of the deceased thanking his mourners, *Tak Tak Tak* represented his friends and family thanking the deceased for his life.

If ever he was to write something it would be much easier, it seemed, if he could construct something within the pages, something useful, but also something mystical. Perhaps he would try to construct a cemetery, a beautiful little Danish cemetery with trellises of doves and love birds crawling on top of the headstones and each of the dead memorialized with the lovely Danish prefix – *Kaene*. "Dear." The cemetery would be an attempt to build something that would be a special gift to the reader. Something that would last, beyond the life of his book, a magical construct.

So again—KAENE MICKEY BERNSTEIN

Fat. Pig-eyed. Shrewd Mickey Bernstein. A cigar always stuck in the side of his mouth. A drunk. Never got out of eighth grade. My uncle. Married to Rose, my father's sister, childless, a barren marriage. Mickey made millions in the *smatteh* business. Dress factories. King of the oversized woman's trade. Blew it all. Not quite. Left Rose enough to have a black Cadillac, a maid and a chauffeur, and a fancy rented apartment at an apartment hotel on the edge of Lincoln Park in Chicago. The chauffeur stole what was left of Rose's money, her diamond pendant disappeared into the projects, Cabrini Green. Her sapphire ring. The black Cadillac went too, her bank accounts, her stock, they ripped at her like piranhas and when nothing was left but a little, old, frightened Jewish lady, mute and alone in her room, they gave her back to her family, her brothers, who supported her until she died.

Mickey Bernstein never lived to see how Rose died. He lived his last days dressed in diapers with Rose as his nurse. Mickey profanely mumbling for a drink through a haze of small strokes. A tough kid out of the west side of Chicago. He used to wear a pink carnation in his lapel, big camel's hair coats and a white broad-brimmed fedora. No kids. Never any kids. A yacht in Florida he named after Rose. In a way I became their child. I remember they gave me a model toy car when I was eight or nine for Chanukah, a Pierce Arrow. A beautiful model of a Pierce Arrow with headlights sculpted in its fenders, whitewalls, and red wheels and a working rumble seat. It was made of heavy metal and I filled in the windows with a light blue-colored wax that I got by melting my mother's candles. The windows were like waxy glass – a gray blue-colored glass that I smoothed with my fingers.

KAENE ROSE LEVIN BERNSTEIN

Mickey's wife, my Aunt Rose. Not like Allen Ginsberg's "Aunt Rose". She didn't have hair on her chin. She was a cosmopolitan woman. She had a lovely singing voice like an opera star. She was a big woman. They were big people, Mickey and Rose. She always wore a black silk dress and posed in photographs in profile so she would look thinner. She also had a big heart. When I had graduated college she gave me a car, a two-door two-toned brown and beige Chevrolet. A brown bottom with a beige top and red wheels. She bought it on her own. Rose never had her own money. Mickey controlled the money doling out a weekly allowance to her. He bought her jewelry in restaurants. It was always "hot" being fenced in whispers by the restaurant's owner. I was with them in "The Singapore" on Rush Street when Mickey bought Rose the star sapphire. She was a consummate nagger and he bought her gifts to keep her quiet. She bought the car on time even though Mickey had at least two million in the bank. She paid for my car secretly each month from her household allowance. I thanked her and used the car to seduce college girls. At least I would try. I hardly ever succeeded. No, I don't think I ever succeeded. No one would go to bed with you even if you had a brand new car given to you by your aunt.

Kaene Elaine Marks

I knew it would happen. The faces of the young women would begin intruding. I can't keep writing without seeing the faces that keep floating into my mind. I really shouldn't put Elaine Marks into my cemetery here in Copenhagen. But I haven't seen her in over forty years and she'll never know. She was a real Jewish beauty. She had dark eyes and dark, long, shining hair that hung straight down from her shoulders and she was very slender. I lied when I said I never succeeded with the car. I think I can say I succeeded often if you can view the car as an accessory to the seduction. Even then, if a place could be found, a room, an apartment, your parents' home, it was much more preferable than the backseat of a car. By putting Elaine Marks in the cemetery I am in a sense handing her the gift of death to protect her identity. She's probably very much alive. I hope she is and I hope she doesn't read this because she was always kind to me, a lovely, kind, intelligent young woman and she doesn't deserve my kind of memorial.

I remember making love to her or at least trying to make love to her. My parents were gone. I lived at home and we had the evening together. No one would bother us. She came home with me in my new car and we got into my bed, naked. No, she wore one of my summer robes, but she was naked underneath the robe. I found an ancient rubber in my top drawer. I was inside of her quickly and she held me back for a moment and said to me, "If we were married, we could do this all the time." Elaine Marks. Perhaps the most beautiful Jewish girl I had ever known. I was twenty-three, she was maybe twenty. I pushed. I was caught in a tight little chamber. I was inside her maybe three or four inches. I didn't realize that I

13

was attempting to make love to a virgin. That she was a virgin. That's how dumb I was, how unskilled at lovemaking. I pushed again and again, but I couldn't break through her maidenhead. I didn't want to hurt her. She was a true virgin, maybe a doctor could do the job. I couldn't. Still, she is pinned by that moment into my memory, the fragrance of the evening, my triumph and yet failure at love.

He closed the notebook and put his pen down. He had no justification for writing about Elaine Marks. Why should he invade her privacy? She was probably a grandmother. He'd heard she was living in Boston. He could just rip up the pages about her. Mickey and Rose, they were beyond caring. Each a pile of bones rotting in a cemetery in Chicago. They weren't even buried together. Mickey was buried with his family, Rose with her family. He should have written about Mickey's trick with his double-jointed toes simulating trench foot, the trick that got him out of the trenches in France in 1917, and his imitation of Jimmy Durante with his teeth. He could add that tomorrow. Tomorrow he'd describe how Mickey would take his teeth out and hold them in his open palm and imitate Durante singing in Durante's mumbling accent, "a one tooth, a whole tooth, a one tooth, a two tooth." He made a few notes in the notebook where he'd stopped, "Mickey – France, imitate Durante, trench foot – double-jointed, 'a one tooth, a whole tooth.' 'Sing Rosie – Sing.'" He would also do a riff on Rose's opera voice. How the brothers would always encourage her to sing. He put the notebook down and went into the bathroom and looked at himself in the mirror. Wisps of gray hair growing over his ears, a mole removed from below his throat leaving a round nickel-sized scar. Thank God it wasn't melanoma. He'd had a friend die of a melanoma on his scalp. He'd discovered it one day in the mirror and six weeks later he was dead.

Kaene/Malcolm Cohen, his dear friend, Mel Cohen. A professor of classic Greek. His own forehead was spotted with tiny lesions and age marks. Which one would darken into Kaene Jonny/Levin? Did Nikos Kazantzakis worry about melanoma? No. He worried about getting laid and loving life. "Report to Greco." Learn to love, Jonny Levin. He looked at himself in the mirror, learn all over again to love.

3

IT'S THE NEXT MORNING. It had been very hard to sleep, so warm in the room because he had to close the windows. Sounds of kids singing in the street and shouting all night after he stopped constructing the little gravestones. At least he'd left Elaine Marks in peace. He hopes he left her in peace. He doesn't know if he can really continue with the history but it seems he's constructed a beginning. A fragile beginning.

So if he's to be Jonny Levin and see more of Copenhagen, he thinks about renting a bicycle this morning. What about it, Jonny Levin? Stop building the cemetery, and get up and out of the room and rent a bicycle.

But first breakfast, and he just makes the 9:30 deadline. The hostess is at the door and is about to close it. A young black woman in a uniform with a white collar and dancing eyes. She seats him with a man and two women. The man looks up at him with a smile and immediately speaks to him in English. The women pay no attention.

"So where are you from fella?" the man asks. "I know you're from the States."

"How do you know?"

"The shoes. I always look at the shoes. You've got American shoes. Hush Puppies."

"Am I wearing American shoes?"

He leans over toward Jonny Levin and picks a piece of thread off of his shirt.

"*Smutz*, you've got a piece of *smutz* there. I got rid of it for you." He flicked at a piece of thread.

The man was about his age in his early sixties. He had a fluid, expressive Jewish face, a long bulbous nose, his cheeks were flushed and a full head of hair brownish and yellowing in a pompadour. He wore an initialed English purple dress shirt with a white round open collar. The shirt was initialed on the breast pocket with his initials "ML" in a circle of laurel leaves and on the white cuffs "ML" in straight cleft letters. His fingernails were immaculately manicured and his thick fingers glistened.

The two ladies, one round faced, the other slim and rather attractive, in their late fifties or early sixties, pretended to be inspecting their menus, but they were watching and listening.

"I didn't get your name."

"Mooney Levine, and yours?"

"Jonny Levin."

"You're Jonny Levine? You're kidding me. Johnny Levine is my nephew. Maybe we're *mishpocheh*? Except Johnny Levine's from Philly and I'm from Manhattan, 89th and Central Park West."

"You really have a nephew named Johnny Levin? How do you spell Levin?"

"L.e.v.i.n.e. Sure. Johnny Levine. He's a dentist in Philly. An oral surgeon"

"We're not related. I spell my name L-e-v-i-n. And I'm

16

from Chicago. Also my first name is J.o.n, not J.o.h.n. What are you doing in Denmark?"

"I sell carnie equipment."

"Carnie equipment?"

"For carnivals. The horses and the chariots in the carousel in Tivoli. They're all mine. Thirty six Jumpers, fourteen Standers, it's the same size as the carousel on Coney Island. Those Coney Island horses are mine too. All my horses are hand-carved in Brooklyn. I sell the most beautiful Jumpers and Standers in the world." Mooney Levine set his coffee aside and pulled a binder of photos up from the floor, put his glasses on and spread the binder on the table. There were glossy color photos of wild-eyed thick-maned carved wooden horses with red-cheeked wooden cavaliers and dirndled wooden maidens with blonde tresses standing as attendants.

"My Jumpers, all pure Lipizzan stallions."

The two women each were giving their orders. They both ordered curried eggs over toast and cold salmon. They were still listening but pretended to be talking about friends they were expecting.

"What's your line of business in Chicago, Jonny?"

"I teach at a university."

"What do you teach?"

"English. English Literature. I'm a professor."

"So you're a professor. Good. How's business?" he asked.

"I'm making a living."

"I'll tell you a little joke, Professor," he held Jonny Levin's arm down on the table. "There's this little Jewish guy in Brooklyn who throws himself in front of a cab and lies there moaning on the street under the wheels. A crowd gathers. One of his friends sees him lying under the cab and rushes over and bends down to help him. 'Irving, Irving, are you all right? What are you doing?'

17

"*Ich machen a leben,*" the little guy says. "You know Yid-dish, Jonny?"

"I know a little."

"*'Ich machen a leben'* means 'I'm making a living.'" Mooney Levine laughs and laughs and then flipped to some more photos.

"I also sell jewelry. Rings. Mens' and womens' costume jewelry. Special rings. Here, watch, I want my check. Now watch the hostess." He was wearing a big clear glass stone on his ring and he caught a slant of sunlight falling across the table with the ring and shined it in the hostess's eye. "Check, Miss," he signalled with a little wave.

"You could hurt that young woman's eye," one of the women said to him. "You really shouldn't do that."

"No, it don't hurt, it just gets their attention."

The hostess brought the check over.

"Did I startle you miss?"

"No, I just suddenly saw this huge flash of light. Do you have some kind of flashlight?"

"No, just this." He flashed the ring around the room, flashing sunlight on the tiered, jellied sardine mold and the plaster cupids along the tops of the heavy drawn maroon velvet drapes.

He signed his bill with a flourish and handed the hostess back her pen as if it were a gift.

"Nice talking to you Professor, ladies. Come over to Tivoli and see my horses. I'll get you on the carousel with a pass. They've got a brass ring machine there. Grab a brass ring and you take home a set of Royal Copenhagen china free."

"I'm renting a bike today."

"So come over tonight, Professor. It's only a few blocks. I've also got my other merchandise in a booth with some Danish ladies. I do a little magic on the side." He flipped to another photo of an emerald-green ring flecked with gold. "That's a séance ring. We've got a séance going on over there tonight at eight. What about it ladies? Want to come to a séance? Here's my card. Bring the Professor. I'll take you all for a carousel ride in the moonlight. Ever ride a giraffe? I've got them too." He flipped his album to a glossy photo of an astonished looking wooden giraffe.

"See you later," he said. Then he was gone, snapping his fingers for the elevators. "*Hiss*," he called, the Danish word for elevator. "Hold that *hiss*."

"That man is really bizarre, very strange," one of the women said after Mooney Levine left the table. "Look at his card."

Mooney F. Levine, New York City, U.S.A. and International Productions, Inc. present a séance tonight at eight. Booth 33 at Tivoli. Josefina, the internationally acclaimed Seeress, will cure your heartache, love, and money problems. Josefina accepts Visa, MasterCard, and American Express. No tape recorders or video cameras. Proven results and testimonials. Modest entrance fee. One free question. Performance in English. Danish translation.,

Her friend looked at the card, pushed her glasses back on her head and continued, "Let's go, Martha. One free question."

"No, first you pay the entrance fee, Elyse."

"No, I don't think so. I think you get a free question and then if you want to stay you pay the entrance fee."

Martha handed the card to Jonny Levin.

She let her glasses fall back on the chain. She was a heavy

woman with an intelligent face and a cultured accent. "You're from Chicago?" she said to him pleasantly. "Where in Chicago?"

"Evanston."

"Oh, Evanston, I have friends there. The Koenigsbergs. Where in Evanston?"

"Near the University."

"Do you know Fred and Enid Koenigsberg?"

The second woman was elegantly slim, in a black slack suit. She had a smooth face with obviously a few cosmetic changes. She wore horn-rimmed glasses on a chain and dressed in a black jacket and a crème-colored cashmere turtleneck sweater. "Do you know Harold and Sally Hechman?" she asked him. Harold practically owns one of the banks in Evanston. I think he's the president of the biggest bank there. I also think he's a trustee of Northwestern. I heard you say you teach at a university. I'm Elyse Friedberg." She extended her hand and he shook it. She was rather sexy. It was perhaps the first time he'd touched a woman since he'd been in Copenhagen.

He wasn't about to tell her where he taught. He didn't want to make American friends in Denmark. These were obviously two wealthy Jewish women from Chicago. He didn't want to play status games with them at breakfast.

"I'm Jonny Levin," he said quietly to Elyse Friedberg. He thought of dropping the "Jonny" with these two American ladies, but he didn't.

"Hello Jonny Levin. A fellow Chicagoan," The heavier woman extended her hand and he shook it. "I'm Martha Selig. Did you say you taught at Northwestern?"

"No I didn't say that."

"Where do you teach?"

"Martha, leave him alone. The man doesn't want to tell where he teaches. He has a reason. So leave it alone."

20

"I just think it's so strange."

Already he was annoyed by her. "Do you have an occupation you want to tell me about?" he asked her.

"Occupation? Hell no. We're just running around Europe. I can't stand Copenhagen. What a provincial town. There's nothing here. Just a square, a few towers and statues, a shopping street, Strøget. Is that what it's called? We're on our way to Stockholm then Helsinki and St. Petersburg. What did we buy here Elyse? I don't even remember."

"You bought some silver at Georg Jensen."

He ordered French toast and some tea.

"Have you been to Tivoli?" he asked them.

"No, but I'd really like to go see that man's production," Elyse Friedberg answered him. "I'd like to go to a séance. I've never been to a séance. I think I'd love it."

"I hate all those yiddishisms he used, Elyse. *Smutz*. What's *smutz*?"

"Dirt," he told her. "*Smutz* is a speck of dirt."

"Can't he just say 'dirt'? What about *mishpocheh*? I know what that means. Family. *Meshugana*? That's what he is. A real New York *meshugana*. He says he sells carnival horses. He runs séances. He's a real New York *meshugana*. I'm not going anywhere near that man, Elyse."

"He said he'd give us each one free question, Martha, and a pass to the carousel."

"That's just what I need. A pass to the carousel. I'm too old to go twirling."

"Martha, where are we going tonight? We let the driver go. We don't have a car. The ballet is closed, the opera is closed. Why not a séance? We can walk over there. It's only a few blocks." She suddenly put her slender hand on top of Jonny Levin's hand with a half-smile. "If you don't have plans, join us."

21

Both women stood up and took their bills. She touched his hand again. "I'll save you a place at the séance table."

She was a direct woman. And she'd given him an invitation. He watched them head into the lobby toward the elevator. She had a graceful walk. Her friend was a busybody, a gossip, but the woman who touched his hand had a certain elegance about her, a kind of graceful elegance in her walk and even in her directness. He turned to his French toast. An interesting woman, but did he really want to hook up in Copenhagen with a woman from Chicago? If she wouldn't intrude on him when they returned it might be nice. He could go into the city occasionally and meet her for theater or perhaps even the opera. It would be better than falling asleep in his chair watching television. He'd been doing a lot of that lately. But not since he'd arrived in Denmark. Not one night asleep in the chair. And he'd finally begun writing again. He looked up and saw Mooney Levine coming out of the elevator and watched him at the front desk where he began talking to the two, young blonde receptionists. They were both laughing with him and he leaned towards them and one of them seemed to sniff his cheek and then she took a white carnation from the vase of flowers on the marble countertop and carefully pinned the flower to his lapel. She did it laughing and tossing her hair. They both then pretended to admire him. He turned and headed towards the dining room. He was dressed in an Italian-cut brown jacket with padded shoulders and a yellow silk ascot. He came directly to Jonny Levin's table.

"How do you do it Mooney?"

"Easy. I just put a little of my cologne on. Just a spritz. It's my own brand. I have it made for me in Paris."

"Cologne?"

"Here's a small sample bottle. On the house. Wear it. The women will never leave you alone. It's got a special chemical in it."

"I couldn't do that."

22

"So be a *putz*. An older man needs a lift. It's the Viagra of the aftershaves. It's got a pheromone in it, like an aphrodisiac."

He set the tiny bottle beside Jonny Levin's plate.

"It's a gift. I'll see you tonight, professor. Wear a few drops of this stuff. The Danish women love it. And here's one more joke." He looked around the dining room to see if anyone was listening and lowered his voice. "A man goes to a doctor for some Viagra, 'Doc, I can't get it up. What should I do?' The doc says, 'Take this Viagra and then call me.' The guy takes it that night and just before he tries to make love to his wife he falls over dead on the couch. She calls the paramedics and they work on him for an hour, but he's dead, and she gets out his best suit and a nice tie and calls the funeral parlor and they come over. They take him back to the funeral home and get him all dressed up and put him in the coffin, but they can't get the coffin closed. Why? It was the Viagra. It killed him but it worked."

"You get it, Professor? He had such a big hard-on that they couldn't get the lid down on him."

He slapped Jonny Levin on the back and pointed to the bottle.

"Put a few drops of my stuff on, *burchik*. Just try it. Only a few drops. You won't be sorry. Here, I'll give you just a little spritz." He removed an inlaid pearl spritzer from inside his jacket and spritzed a touch on his index finger and chucked Jonny Levin under the chin. "Just a drop, Professor. It don't take much. If you put on too much it becomes like a repellant. The women start running away. So just a touch, under the chin, behind the ears, on the wrists. You work it out."

He set the inlaid spritzer on the table and gave it to Jonny Levin. "Mother of pearl made for me in Indonesia. It's yours. I get them by the gross. Keep it. There's a war on there, but they still make good spritzers. They make them out of abalone shells."

He chucked Jonny Levin under the chin again, punched

23

him lightly on the shoulder and turned and walked out of the dining room.

4

HE RENTED A BICYCLE. He found a small shop near Radhus Pladsen, the main square of Copenhagen. Radhus was the old red brick tower City Hall. The main square surrounding it was filled with people, lines of tourists, families, water fountains with people sitting on the edges their faces to the sunlight. There were small crowds in circles around the street performers. Also Kierkegaard's gray stone house, very large and formal. Kierkegaard must have come from a wealthy family. As he tried to become more in control of his bicycle, he thought of a line of Kierkegaard that he always gave to his students, "Life can only be understood backwards, but it must be lived forwards." No time for philosophy in the middle of this square. He almost ran over a woman looking at her guidebook, just wobbled around her. He'd rented an old comfortable black bicycle, a woman's bike with three gears, a large straw basket, a bell, handbrakes and a low soft seat and thick tires. He felt quite comfortable on it. It had cost thirty kroner, about three dollars, for the afternoon.

As he rode carefully toward the edge of the square, he thought about the bicycles he'd owned in his life. The first, when he was a boy about ten, was a "Shelby Flyer". It had shiny aluminum fenders, thick balloon tires and a streamlined light built into its front fender. He grew up in Glencoe on Chicago's North Shore. His father owned a small stamping plant that sold parts to the automotive industry. His father was a successful businessman

24

who bought everything for his family wholesale, and the "Shelby Flyer" was a proud gift to his ten year old son. The son wanted a lightweight, thin-tired bike, like his friends' bikes, not a fat-tired heavy aluminum-fendered bike with an aero-flow light built into the fender. In eighth grade and in high school and in his teens, there was a black Schwinn, finally a thin-tired fast bike with a three-speed gearshift. It was also bought wholesale and picked up by father and son at a Chicago freight yard on Roosevelt Road in a packing crate. It took two weeks to assemble and he'd used it for five years, to ride to school, to play baseball, basketball, hockey, and most importantly, to visit girlfriends at night. He was a man about town on a bicycle, like Saroyan's Messenger. He couldn't remember the name of Saroyan's book with the bicycle messenger engraved into the cover. No it wasn't on the cover, it was drawn as one of the chapter headings and the name of the book was "The Bicycle Rider of Beverly Hills". Saroyan's Messenger was drawn as a boy on a bike wearing a Western Union uniform. After reading Saroyan's book, he'd foolishly tried his hand at being a Western Union boy and delivered telegrams during the Korean war. But when the death messages began to come he quit, and put his bicycle away for the rest of high school. Then when he went to college in Champaign after the war, there was the old red bike, a used bike that he rented from a campus bike shop. It was sort of a maroon color. He tried to remember it, but he could only dimly see it lying on its side at a bike rack. No more bicycles until he was a young married man. He bought a suburban Schwinn with a child's seat, and used to ride the children after dinner. The dog, a black Lab, running ahead of them. She would disappear and he could never see her, but he could hear her padded swift footsteps in the suburban darkness and the light tinkling sound of her collar.

He parked the bike at a small sidewalk café and sat down

and ordered coffee. He felt good, proud to have bicycled confidently across the square, and now sitting in the Danish sunlight, closed his eyes for a moment and put on his sunglasses. Poor Saroyan. Whatever happened to him? He used to teach Saroyan in his short story course. "The Bicycle Rider of Beverly Hills," "My Name is Aram," "The Daring Young Man on the Flying Trapeze". He hadn't read any Saroyan in years. Could he name another Armenian writer? There was Michael Arlen, a fine essayist. He used to write for the New Yorker. He hadn't seen anything by Michael Arlen for several years. Michael Arlen's father was Harold Arlen who wrote, "The Green Hat," one of the most popular novels of the '20s. He'd never read "The Green Hat". He would never read "The Green Hat". Was it true that Stalin's wife had been reading it a few weeks before she committed suicide? According to their daughter, Svetlana, that was true. Didn't Stalin partially blame his wife's suicide on Arlen? And then who gave her the pistol? A member of the Inner Circle? Who was it? He had Svetlana Stalin's book, "Thirty Letters to a Friend", in his library at home. If he was home, he could easily look it up. He'd actually seen Svetlana once. She lived in Wisconsin south of Madison where Frank Lloyd Wright had built Taliesen East. He and the children and Magdalena, his first wife, had spent a weekend there. They went to see Chekov's "The Cherry Orchard" in an outdoor arena and just before the lights dimmed, two young ushers seated a heavy set older woman with a round Russian face in her sixties. She was seated across the stage, and when he saw her as the lights went on he realized at once that it was Svetlana. He recognized her from her photo on the cover of her book. He knew that she had married the architect in charge of Taliesen East and she was living there. So he'd come full circle. Armenian writers, Harold Arlen, "The Green Hat" and finally Stalin's daughter Svetlana Alliluyeva. He could have given a lecture on Armenian writers.

26

He'd left out Elia Kazan's "America, America". He smiled at his list making and his didactism.

Now his coffee came and he drank it and began to watch the crowds of people. There was a soccer game between Denmark and the Netherlands. People were walking through the square on their way to the soccer game dressed in their country's colors. The Danes in red and white soccer shirts, some in red tams with white tassels or red oversized stovepipe hats that they would bow to the Dutch in mock greetings. The Dutch wore red, white and blue, the colors of the Dutch tri-color, many also in the tall, silly hats or carrying paper streamers they would toss. Some wore rubber masks of their favorite players. As they passed each other there would be occasional bursts of song and cheering.

There were some street performers moving along the edges of the tables and they stopped almost in front of him. There were two women, one was dancing, a pretty young woman dressed in a black cutaway with a cane and a black silk top hat and a formal white shirt and bow tie. She tipped her hat to him and began to dance in front of him. She apparently recognized he was an American. She began singing in English, "I'm a Very Stylish Woman". She bowed and tapped his table with her cane. Suddenly she put her cheek against his and whispered in his ear, "I'm a Very Stylish Woman". Then she quickly moved away and danced around several of the other tables. Her companion was a tall, blonde woman in her late twenties dressed in a full Indian head-dress, a war bonnet. She was quite beautiful, full breasted, wearing a flesh colored bikini top and a blue velvet jacket as she played the accordion.

She also swayed toward him and put her cheek up against his and whispered to him, "Hello, mister".

What was it? One minute he was sitting in the sunlight brooding about Armenian writers and Stalin's daughter. Now two

Danish beauties were dancing and swaying in front of him. The one with the accordion almost sat down on his lap. "Do you have a request sir?" she asked him smiling and laughing with her friend.

"What kind of request?"

"A song of course. A favorite song."

"Do you know 'Lady of Spain'?"

"Oh, come on sir, that's not our kind of song. You're a sophisticated gentleman and you smell delicious."

"Do I really?"

"Inge, did you notice the gentleman's aftershaving lotion? Do you think he's a movie star from America? Are you in the cinema sir?"

Inge twirled over to him and put her cheek against his again and sniffed.

"Oh he does. He smells delicious."

She held her cane horizontally and did a little swaying shuffle. "He looks like an American movie star or perhaps a director or producer. You will want both of us in your film, won't you?"

She put her top hat down in front of her by having it roll down her arm and they both bowed to the audience. The open hat on the ground was a gesture to him and the others that they would like some money dropped in it.

The people at adjoining tables put some coins in it and began to applaud.

He reached for his billfold and put a twenty kroner note in her hat.

"Oh thank you sir, 'I'm a Very Stylish Woman'," the dancer sang in her husky voice and tapped his shoulder with her cane. She danced over to the adjoining café. The blonde with the accordion followed her and waved goodbye to him and blew him a kiss and gave him a shake of her hips and began playing "Ta Ra Ra Boom Dee-ay". They both began dancing in unison doing

28

bumps and grinds like in the old lithographs of the dancing cabaret girls in the cabarets of Tivoli.

Another woman approached him, a woman in her forties with long brown hair and a very sad ivory oval face. She was holding up a scissors and she wore a placard board around her neck with several black paper silhouettes pasted on the board. She was a silhouette artist and she stood before him and held her scissors up and began cutting a silhouette of his face. She said nothing to him and as she worked she leaned toward him so that her hair brushed his cheek as she moved to one side of his face, and then the other, cutting solemnly and without expression. Then she handed him a finished silhouette of himself in profile.

"Thank you," he said. He held it up to the sunlight. "Thank you very much."

She took the figure back and turned toward him frowning, her hair brushing his face again, and then she snipped off a fragment, a tiny sliver of paper and gave the silhouette back to him.

She said something to him in Danish in a soft voice.

"I'm sorry, I don't speak Danish. I'm an American. Do you speak English?"

"Yes sir, I speak English. Not too well though. Would you care to buy my silhouette? One hundred kroner, sir." She seemed to be slightly smiling at him and then she lapsed back into her somber expression. She had lovely planes to her face and dark eyelashes and pale blue, almost green eyes.

"It's very nice."

"If you like it then you should buy it."

"What will I do with a silhouette?"

"You could frame it. I carry frames in my shop." She quickly handed him a card. "Beautiful frames. You should visit my shop, it's quite near here.

He reached in his pocket and found a hundred kroner

note and handed it to her. The silhouette was about ten dollars. "You're very talented."

"Thank you sir," she said. She looked at him again for a moment and then began moving alongside the adjoining tables holding her scissors up to the customers.

He glanced at her card.

Marguerite Berenstyne

24 Helgoland, Brunsdrata 24
Silhouette Artiste
Berenstyne Frame Shoppe & Antiquaries
Telephone   721-1390

Suddenly she returned to him and in a moment cut out a swan and handed it to him, leaning in again toward him and then turning her back and snipping something and turning away again. She then handed him a white rabbit and turned abruptly and walked toward the next tables. She said nothing to him as she handed him the new cuttings. In five seconds she had produced a beautiful swan with a tail spread in a fan and a rabbit with long ears cut precisely and evenly. She was a master artist and also a dancer as she cut her silhouettes and whirled at first toward him, handing him her gifts, and then turning away and moving down along the other tables.

He looked at the figure of the white swan. It made him remember the small inn he'd stayed in, "The White Swan", in northwestern Holland with Magdalena, who was born in Belgium and had led him on a bicycle trip to Holland. He remembered "The White Swan" in Raalte, with its old feather beds and dormer windows overlooking the square with plane trees and a horse fountain. When they went down for breakfast in the dining room, they faced a scene right out of Rembrandt. Old men in black caps, jackets and trousers, wearing wooden shoes and smoking clay pipes. He hadn't thought of that tiny inn in Holland in years, but suddenly the silhouette of the swan she handed him brought him back to Magdalena and their trip to Holland just before their marriage. He usually tried not to think of her because it would bring back only bad memories. But this was a good memory, almost a tableau of Rembrandt. They had hot chocolate and carried the tray of hot chocolate back upstairs to the feather beds and drank it and made love.

He carefully folded the swan and the rabbit and put them in his wallet. He paid his bill and then rode his bicycle back to the bike rental shop and turned the bike in and walked back to the hotel.

5

BACK AT THE HOTEL he stopped at the counter and asked if he had any mail or messages. The two young lovely blondes were on duty. Very crisp and efficient in their black bow ties and black waistcoats with gold crossed keys pinned in the lapels. They wore white plastic name tags, Dagne and Karen. Both greeted him. There was a bowl of apples on the desk and he thought of taking an apple, but he was afraid he'd break his lower bridge if he tried to bite down. Then he remembered he had a tiny knife in his shaving kit, so he took a green apple. He searched the numbered cubicles behind the counter for a message. He couldn't see well enough to make out his room number and he bent toward Dagne who suddenly leaned in toward him with a pink carnation in her hand and held the flower up to him. "Thank you," he said. *Tak.*

She replied, *Tak,* and brushed her hair back with one hand and turned and searched his cubicle and said in perfect English, "No messages, Mr. Levin, but now instead you have our flower."

"Yes, a pink one. I saw that you gave the other Mr. Levin a white one this morning."

"Oh yes, the other gentleman from America. Also a Mr. Levin but he has added an 'e' to his name, Mr. Levine." She sniffed and leaned in toward him again. "Yours is pink, though, for the afternoon our flowers are always pink. Isn't that true Karen?"

"What?"

"Pink flowers for our guests in the post-noon."

"Yes, that is true."

"So, Mr. Levin without an 'e', your key. Here it is and please have a pleasant evening." She handed him his key and touched his hand, like Elyse Friedberg. Now two women in Copenhagen had touched his hand. He was keeping score.

Again, the elevator ascending and behind the barred cage he held the green stem of the single pink carnation and twisted it under his nose. "*Tak. Tak.* Jonny Levin," he said to himself as the ancient cage climbed up to his floor.

In the room he put his carnation in an empty Coke bottle that he filled with water.

There were some remnants of petunias on the small balcony. He opened the sliding door to let fresh air into the room. The glass panel of the door was filthy. Absolutely scabrous and filthy. He hadn't noticed it behind the brocade curtain, but the glass was dulled with grime and he filled a cup of water and took the Kleenex box from the bathroom and began to clean the door panel. He wasn't doing a very good job though, he barely made a dent in the city grime and only succeeded in making whirlpools on the window. He thought of calling the front desk. What would Dagne and Karen think of Mr. Levin without an 'e' if he immediately called to complain about Copenhagen's grime after receiving a pink carnation? No, he wouldn't call. He stepped out on the balcony. He could see the towers of the old city in the distance. Some of the Dutch soccer fans were on the street alongside the hotel that led to Tivoli. They were shouting and pumping their fists. Several of the women wore the tri-color red, white and blue Dutch flag as capes. The Dutch must have beaten the Danes.

He took a shower and used several of the small plastic bottles of skin gel and conditioner the hotel had provided. After showering and using the bath gel, he realized he had washed away Mooney Levine's pheromone. It was probably just nonsense, this Viagra of aftershave lotions, but just as one final touch after he changed, he took Mooney's abalone shell sprayer and gave himself a little spritz. He felt refreshed after the shower and put on his navy sports coat with brass buttons, almost the uniform of the middle-aged American tourist in Europe. He wore a bright red patterned tie. With the red tie, he looked like a member of Bush's cabinet. They all wore red ties. None of them, though, would spritz themselves with a pheromone after shave or be on their way to a séance. None of them would have been invited to a séance, and with their red power ties, none of them would ever be invited to a séance. Was there one Jew in Bush's Cabinet? He couldn't think of one. The former Press Secretary was a Jew, Ari Fleisher, but he'd resigned, probably to write a book. Just as a precaution, he dropped a Viagra pill into his pillbox. There was something about the woman from Chicago, the thin woman, her invitation to him, her hand on his hand, even the sound of her voice that told him that he would not only need Mooney's cologne, but also the reassurance of the hidden blue

33

pill. He dropped it in his pillbox hidden in his pocket. It was like a *pushkeh*. A Yiddish word for a little hidden purse. He also folded three Danish one hundred kroner notes into a small wad and hid them in the secret compartment of his billfold. Now he had his own *pushkeh*.

Except if he really wanted a *pushkeh*, he should take along not only the Viagra pill, but a condom. He'd bought a new six-pack of condoms on impulse in the O'Hare washroom. A horny middle-aged Jewish professor on sabbatical doesn't enter Denmark without a six-pack of condoms. A six-pack of thin, rubber French condoms with a cover on the package of a beautiful young couple embracing beneath a cascading waterfall.

He hadn't attempted making love to anyone in six months. There'd been a drunken failure six months ago with a teaching assistant in her mid-forties in his department who was as drunk as he was and when he didn't have a condom, she refused to have sex with him unless he went out and bought one and a pack of cigarettes. But he couldn't really get it up anyway, so when he came back to her fortieth-floor apartment, all he'd bought was a pack of cigarettes instead of condoms. She took the cigarettes and pushed him out the door. Now every time he saw her in the corridors or at a staff meeting she avoided him. Since his divorce from Ramona a year ago, that sad, drunken night was his only attempt at sex. When at three in the morning he'd gone for the condoms to an all night drug store on Rush Street, he'd had a premonition that she might attempt to jump out of her apartment window. She was very depressed. She'd been talking about suicide. As he left the apartment he could barely see her outlined in the darkness of the room, her head tilted back on the window pane, the ember glowing from her cigarette, "This is my last cigarette, John. I need some cigarettes, please get me a pack of Winstons." So he'd come back with the cigarettes, but not the condoms and she'd pushed him out the door. After that night he went to a urologist and got a prescription for Viagra. So he'd not only come to Denmark with a box of French condoms, he had a bottle of Viagra pills to go with his new identity.

Before he left on his trip, he received a note from her. It was in a small, white gift envelope, with a white card stuck into his office mail slot. "Bon voyage, John, from your friend – Patricia Bregemann." She'd put the envelope under a rubber band that held a scroll, Lewis Carroll's "Jabberwocky" in Danish also translated into English in alternate paragraphs. A strange going away gift. He'd brought the scroll along to Denmark. Now as he added a French condom to the secret billfold compartment he went to his suitcase and found the tightly-rolled scroll of "Jabberwocky". He read some lines aloud.

> "Min so°n, pas godt på Jabberwock!
> Han river, og hans tand er hvas."
> "Beware the Jabberwock, my son!
> The jaws that bite, the claws that catch!"

Maybe he should take it along to read to Elyse Friedberg. Or at least he could try to memorize the two lines and say them to the desk clerks as he left. But he left the scroll in the room.

When he went downstairs he was quite pleased with himself. He skipped the elevator cage and instead took the stairway down to the lobby. He'd have to learn to count in Danish so he could count the stairs. One of the men in his department had a pedometer that he always wore and did three miles a day. It was a tiny blue belt pedometer and when you pushed a button it announced the number of steps you'd taken. He didn't really need a pedometer. His walking was good. He could bicycle. His aim was steady at the shooting booth. He was beginning to relax. He wasn't certain about the cemetery construction. Maybe he'd give that up, but at least he'd begun writing again. He didn't stop at the desk in the lobby to go through the charade with the two young women. Anyway, they were registering some new arrivals. As he entered the street, the Danish night seemed fragrant and a soft wind blew on his cheek. And then he spotted her, a young Danish prostitute approaching him as he passed the tavern next to the hotel.

"Sir, are you looking for a companion," she called to him in English.

She was about twenty, maybe twenty-two, dressed in a black tank top with a head of black curls. She wobbled toward him on heavy black platform shoes. She was thin and ungainly, very pale, younger than his youngest daughter, and she had a jewel in her navel, a black faceted jewel. She also had a ring clipped to her left ear with a tiny companion black jewel, lavender toenails, a tiny black shoulder purse, and a red string of ribbon underneath her hair. She was quite exotic, even beautiful, like a young hawk descending on him from the night and landing at his feet. She was smoking and she flipped the cigarette away and asked him again, "Do you, sir, want a companion for the evening?" She spoke English with an unusual accent. "I am a licensed guide. I can show you Copenhagen."

"Where are you from?" he said to her.

"What difference does it make where I am from? You're an American, no? Or maybe an Englishman, a London man? I can tell from your clothes and you're speaking English. I am from Lithuania, if that should make a difference. Now, does it make a difference? Have you heard of Lithuania?"

"I am not looking for a companion."

"Oh, that is a pity. Do you think I am a streetwalker? Is that what you think? I am a guide and a commission agent. I will take you shopping. You seem like a gentleman. Are you really from America? Most Americans come in the summer, not in spring."

"Yes, I'm an American."

"And you're here in Denmark as a visitor?"

"Yes."

"So I can show you Copenhagen. It's a beautiful city. I have excellent connections. I will be your guide. Have you been to the casino at the Radisson? We can take a taxi and have dinner there."

She held his wrist and looked down the street for a taxi. She was the third woman who'd touched him in Denmark. Elyse Friedberg, Karen at the hotel desk, and now this young Lithuanian woman. He was still keeping score. He should have a pedometer that counted the touches, a pedometer with a button you could push that would announce the number of women who had touched your wrist.

"Where are you from in America?"

"I'm from Chicago."

"I shall visit there someday." She was quite tall, about three or four inches taller than him. Even without her platform shoes she would be taller. She wore tiny square-shaped snap-on sunglasses that reflected green. She also wore wire-rimmed glasses underneath the sunglasses.

She pointed to the stairs that led down to a tavern.

"Let's go downstairs and have a drink and discuss our situation."

"No, I'm not interested in having a drink and we don't have a situation."

"Where are you going?"

"I'm going to Tivoli."

"Well, then I'll be your guide to Tivoli. I am a licensed, commission agent for Royal Copenhagen. We will visit their showroom and then we will visit the ballet. It's an outdoor ballet. We can stand in the garden and watch Pierrot together. I am

37

also an official guide for the ballet. I will show you my pass. Then to the swan boats. And then we will take a swan boat to a restaurant for dinner. I am connected to several excellent restaurants."

She pulled on his wrist and began to lead him down the street. Her thumb and index finger each had a glass ring and she wore a heavy silver flanged cross around her neck. Also she leaned her head against his shoulder as they walked.

"You're wearing a lovely cologne, sir. Are you a married gentleman?"

"No I'm not married, I'm a divorced gentleman." If he really wanted to open himself up to a new experience, this could be one. She was forty years younger and probably a prostitute and not a guide for Royal Copenhagen or the ballet. Yet the prospect of eating boiled potatoes and herring again by himself wasn't so compelling that he could tell this young woman to get lost.

"What do you charge for your guided tour?" he asked her.

"Well I charge nothing for Royal Copenhagen. If you buy something I receive a commission from the store. The ballet is also without charge. We will just stand at the rear. The swan boat is also free. The dinner is at your expense and I will also eat, but there is no charge for my meal, the restaurant will pay for me."

"So the entire time with you is free?"

She laughed. "Yes, absolutely free. Can you believe it as a capitalist? Americans are always worried about money. That is why you have so much. You are such a rich and powerful country. I do not worry about money. I am a free spirit. That is why I have so little, but I am a free spirit. My spirit is free. Is your spirit free sir?"

"No, I don't think my spirit is free."

They were within a block of Tivoli. He could see the strings of white bulbs outlining the wooden towers and the parachute rides looming up down the street. There were silk-screened

38

banners on the lamp posts advertising a Chinese opera from Peking. She guided him across the street through the roundabout of traffic, ignoring the cars, pointing at one to stop, and then crossing to the curb.

"You will have no need for a ticket to Tivoli, sir. You are with me." She smiled at the two young attendants at the ticket booth, both dressed in dark navy braided jackets with gold buttons, like the King's Guards.

"See, you're perfectly welcome here as my guest and there is Royal Copenhagen." She pointed to the entrance of the showroom and opened the door.

She was immediately met by the manager, a fat-faced, red-cheeked blonde balding man. He wore a dark blue suit and vest and a red and blue striped tie with tiny Danish crowns.

"I have brought you a customer, a gentleman from America."

"How nice to see you sir. You are most welcome to our showroom." The manager looked at her rather skeptically.

"I will show the gentleman around. I am quite familiar with the store."

"You are very welcome sir." The man bowed his head and smiled and walked to another section of the store without saying anything further.

"They also have beautiful glassware here as well as china." She pointed to the department in the other room. "Crystal and glass lined with silver, also lead goblets. May I ask your name sir?"

"Jonny."

"You also have a last name?"

"Jonny Levin."

"My name is Leda, like Leda and the Swan. My last name is too complicated." She laughed and bowed and spread her arms in an exaggerated imitation of a swan. As she bowed her purse swung out and hit a china sugar bowl and pitcher set and knocked them off their pedestal. They both shattered as they hit the tile floor.

"Oh, sweet Jesus, what have I done now?"

"You are a rather clumsy swan, Leda."

"Oh, dear Jesus. I'm so sorry. I am always foolish. This will cost me a fortune. I cannot pay for these." She pushed her sunglasses up on her head and began to pick up the pieces. "Oh, these poor angels. They'll never fly again."

The shattered pieces were blue ceramic angels painted on Italian ceramic earthenware. "I've broken their wings. I've shattered their wings. Did you see their eyes? You can see how angry they are at me."

"They didn't look angry to me. They looked happy. How would you like to spend your whole life painted on a bowl. Now they can just fly away."

"They can't fly away with broken wings. Let's just leave. I'll take the pieces with me. I have a friend who will fix them."

She turned quickly and took his wrist again and led him toward the door and then outside to the gravel paths edged by flower beds.

"Are we just sneaking out without paying for them. I don't think that's very honest Leda."

"Honesty is a relative thing, Mr. American, depending on the size of your purse. We'll walk to the ballet now. I will have these pieces repaired by my friend. She's a master with ceramics. I will return the angels with their wings put back together."

"You speak excellent English, Leda. Where did you learn to speak English?"

"I studied for several years. When I started school at the Lycee, as children in Lithuania we were taught Russian. It was compulsory. But when we broke away from Russia and won our freedom, English was taught in the Gymnasium and I became an advanced student of English."

"Where are you from in Lithuania?"

"I'm from Kaunas. Do you know Kaunas? It is the second largest city in Lithuania next to Vilnius, the capital city."

"Yes, I know both Kaunas and Vilnius."

"Over there is the ballet." She pointed at a crowd standing in front of a small stage in a grove of trees strung with colored lights. There was an orchestra playing and a performer dressed as a Harlequin in a yellow and blue costume and a lace collar dancing with a black mask over his eyes and wearing a black tri-corner hat. He looked exactly like a Picasso Harlequin.

She took his hand and led him to the rear. "That's Pierrot," she said her eyes flashing up at him as she leaned back against him. Her body felt hard and thin and he sensed the fragrance of her hair brushing against his face as she leaned back against him and they watched Pierrot dancing to Swan Lake. He almost put his hands around her waist as she nestled her body against him and he felt the warmth of her bare shoulders on his chest. The performance was quite lovely, very simple. The solo performer was Pierrot as a Harlequin dancing gracefully to Tchaikovsky. He would have to watch himself with this young woman. He was surprised that in just a few moments of touching up against her he was already filled with longing and so attracted by her fragrance, the touch of her skin and her laughter. He didn't move away from her.

"Now to the swan boats," she said turning. "The swan boats are over there. They have just begun operating for the season" She pointed to a lagoon filled with children and parents. Danish couples with their children were riding in motorized boats with carved swans as prows moving through a lagoon of castles and waterwheels, Chinese pagodas and miniature waterfalls. The

41

children were mostly high-crowned little blonde boys and girls who wore enormous silken hair ribbons and knit sweaters, steering proudly beside their fathers and mothers.

Suddenly he realized that he'd become enveloped in an intoxicating mixture of swans – first the memory of The White Swan, the inn in Raalte in the Netherlands with Magdelena. Then Leda the swan girl from Lithuania with the shattered angels in her purse. The Harlequin Pierrot dancing to Swan Lake and now the astonished laughter of children guiding the swan boats through the ancient lagoon.

"Do you always commandeer a swan boat when you want to escape Royal Copenhagen, Leda?"

"Always."

She already had the hawser in her hand and held the boat steady against the pier. She knew the young man in charge of the boats who stood watching her. He wore a straw Venetian gondolier's hat.

"Get in, Jonny Levin, and I will hold the boat for you."

She steered them carefully through the boats of children and their parents, occasionally bumping one of them and saying, "*Unskold*", "Excuse me", and smiling at the parents. She steered them away from the pack of boats to a clear channel in the lagoon. She was a skilled swan boat operator. When they reached the channel she turned and put his hand on the tiller and moved behind him.

"Just steer a straight course to the restaurant. You can see it down there. The one with the blue awning and all the flags."

So here he was, steering a swan boat under the stars and with a secret *pushkeh* in his back pocket filled with mysterious oddments all unknown to this young Leda. He took the tiller.

"You know Leda," he said pointing to a constellation, "there are Leda's two twin sons, Pollex and Castor. The two brightest stars."

She looked up as he pointed and then she reached over

his shoulder and held the tiller with her hand over his hand and her lips on the back of his neck.

"You really have this marvelous cologne, Jonny Levin. I seem to want to put my arms around you."

They were passing several swan boats with parents and children coming in the opposite direction. She squeezed a rubber bulb at the nape of the swan's neck and blew a horn at them which approximated the claxon bray of a swan and the children screeched and were delighted. All this with her lips still pressed against his neck and their boat rocking in the channel in the wake of the passing boats.

Now he could feel the touch of her mouth against his ear as she steered over him with her hand on top of his hand.

"You also had a daughter named 'Helen', 'Helen of Troy'. The Trojan War was fought over her. She was stolen by the Trojan king."

"I know," she said into his ear. "They brought that big wooden horse to rescue her. Steer carefully Jonny Levin. You sound like a school teacher. Are you a teacher?" She put her lips on his ear again.

"Turn right Jonny Levin. Right into that little passageway there beside that pier with the Danish flags."

She suddenly crawled onto the bow of the boat and crouched and took the coil of rope.

"The lever on your left, move it down."

He did as he was told and they began to glide into the dock and she jumped off the bow onto the pier and tied them to a cleat.

"Now there'll be a big bump and my American teacher friend will be careful."

He stepped out of the boat carefully and adjusted his blue jacket and his tie and wiped the spray off his shoulders. "Leda, what do you know about Helen of Troy?"

"I know I am not Helen of Troy. Leda is the mother of Helen. Helen of Troy is my daughter."

"Yes, you're right."

"I know that legend. I am most of the time right."

"I've noticed that."

"Also I am totally attracted to your alluring cologne."

"I've also noticed that. But, I think off the swan boat I won't be so alluring."

"I don't understand."

"I mean, are you really attracted to older men on land, Leda, not just at sea? I can understand the attraction on a sea voyage, but now back on land I doubt if it will last."

"You will buy me dinner and we will see. You are not an ordinary older man. Also you are not so old. There is something very mysterious about you, some secret. I will find it."

The hostess smiled at them as they approached her and said something in Danish to Leda which he presumed was "Good Evening." She led them to a small table that faced open French doors and the lagoon. She lit a candle and held the chair for him. He thanked her, but instead took his jacket off and put it over Leda's shoulders and held her chair. The hostess watched without expression and still held his chair. She was a slim woman in a white nylon blouse, black jacket, and long black skirt, a high cheekboned Danish blonde in her forties. She picked up and held the large menus against her breasts and her eyes seemed to engage his with both amusement and Danish formality.

She asked him in English if they would like something to drink.

He saw the two men at the table across from them drinking Carlsberg beer and chasers of Aquavit.

"Leda, would you like what they're drinking? Do you like beer?"

"I love the Danish beer, Carlsberg. It's not too strong. Very pleasant."

"Then bring us just the same combination that the two men are having, a bottle of Carlsberg beer for each of us and a bottle of Aquavit and two shot glasses." He felt that he sounded like Victor Borge. A paternalistic Victor Borge ordering drinks for his daughter. Borge was a Danish Jew so there would be some validity assuming Borge's manner.

When the hostess left the table, she touched his hand. He'd add that gratuitous gesture to his hand touching count.

A young waitress brought them a tray with two bottles of Carlsberg and a blue bottle of Aquavit. He poured a glass of beer for each of them. He looked at the bottle of Carlsberg "by appointment of the Danish royal court". He turned the green bottle and pointed to the crown on the label.

"Is that crest the Danish royal crown?"

"I don't know, but Carlsberg is very popular beer here. The most popular. The most favorite." She raised her glass of beer to him and licking the foam off her lips as she drank she said, *Skål* to him.

"*Skål?* Is that the Danish drinking toast?"

"Yes it is. The same as 'Cheers'."

"They also say *Skål* when you win at roulette."

"Oh, I didn't know that. *Skål* at roulette?"

"Only when you win. They say nothing when you lose."

"You are a winner at roulette?"

"I only win one kroner pieces. I have a bag full of one kroner coins."

"Are you a wealthy man in America? If you're a school teacher you must not be too wealthy. The teachers in Lithuania are very poor."

"I am a school teacher and I'm not a wealthy man."

"I need to borrow some money from you Jonny, even if

you are not a wealthy man. I need four thousand kroner. I have to have it tonight."

"I don't lend money."

"I need desperately to borrow money."

"Have you some collateral?"

"Collateral, of course. What is that?" She filled each of their shot glasses with a shot of Aquavit from the blue bottle and held her beer glass up to him. "Skål." She held one finger up and motioned him to drink the shot down in one swallow.

"Collateral is security for a debt, like a mortgage on a house. Do you know what a mortgage is?"

He took a sip of the Aquavit while she stared at him. It was very strong and tasted like ouzo or slivovitz.

"This is very good. Good and strong."

"Just swallow it down in one swallow like I did. You don't just touch it with the tongue, you take it down like this." She poured herself another shot and held it up to him. "Skål." She gestured at him again to drink and held up two fingers.

He drank his shot down and felt it searing his throat and then burning in his stomach.

"No I can't loan you four thousand kroner. You're trying to get me drunk. Why do you need four thousand kroner?"

"To pay my room rent. Otherwise my landlady will put my things on the street tonight. She told me that when I left. Not to come back without four thousand kroner."

"And you expect me to pay your rent? You probably say that to every man you meet."

"That's cruel. It's not true. I only ask you because I can see that you're a gentleman. A gentleman will always help a lady if the lady truly needs his help. I truly need your help."

She bent her head down and shook her hair out and took off the heavy silver cross she wore on a leather thong around her neck and handed it to him. "This cross will be my security, or what you call collateral."

"I don't want your cross."

"I insist. It is my most precious possession. It was given to me by an elderly priest in Vilnius before I left Lithuania. Father Jelinskaitas. He blessed it and told me it would always protect me. I will give it to you and put it around your neck as a symbol of my honesty." She poured them each another shot of Aquavit and filled his beer glass.

"Drink up – *Skål*. She clicked their glasses." It was her third shot and his second. She held up three fingers and held her nose and tossed her shot down.

"Just hold your nose and close your eyes like I do and drink it down, Jonny Levin."

He tried her technique and again he could feel the shot burning its way down into his stomach and he put his hand over his glass. Why was he drinking like this?

"No more Leda. We've got to order something. Some bread, some herring, some appetizers, some potatoes." He looked around for the waitress.

Suddenly Leda stood up and moved in back of him and put her arms around him. She dropped the necklace with the heavy cross over his neck.

"Now you have what you call my collateral and you will be like my priest and protect me."

The two men opposite them stopped their drinking and began watching them.

"I won't give you the money Leda. Sit down. Also I don't want your cross." He reached back and took it off and dropped it on her plate.

She staggered back to the table and sat down. "I'm already drunk. You're such a mean man. Why do you let me get this way? You have made me drunk and dizzy."

She dropped the cross around her neck again and stood up. "I can't understand you. A wealthy American. You are so selfish. Wealthy and selfish. I will have to go back on the street and find someone else."

She stood for a moment looking at him and put one of the rolls in her purse and turned and walked away through the tables without looking back at him. Suddenly she turned and came back and took his jacket off and put it over his shoulders.

"I can't take your coat even if you're selfish. I am not a thief. Here it is. Thank you for letting me wear it."

She stumbled against the table.

"Sit down," he said to her. "Sit down Leda."

"I won't sit."

He put his hand out to her and pulled her down.

"Sit down and listen to me."

"I don't have to listen to you."

"How can you expect me to pay your rent? We've known each other for one hour."

"And we have learned a lot about each other." She tossed her hair. "Haven't we, Mr. American?"

"Don't call me Mr. American."

"I have learned that you will not help me. I cannot rely on you. What do you think I am, a prostitute? A street walker? I am not a prostitute. I am a licensed tour guide and physical therapist. If you give me the money I will come to your room and massage you or make an appointment for you and you can come to my studio. If I still have a studio. The landlady has probably put my things on the street."

"I don't want a massage."

She tried to pour herself another shot of Aquavit but he held the bottle away from her.

"All right. I won't massage you. I will just manipulate you. I can see you have very poor posture."

"I have a back problem."

"I will very gently manipulate your back. Where is the problem, upper or lower?"

The young waitress came now with a tray of appetizers, different types of herring and sliced bread and tiny boiled red potatoes.

"I have a lovely studio with all the equipment, candles and oils and fragrances, but I am about to lose all my possessions. I am a desperate woman. Can't you see that?" Tears were glistening on her cheeks.

"All right, I'll help you Leda. But I won't give you four thousand kroner, that's four hundred dollars. I will give you only what I have and I'll buy you a dinner."

"What do you have?"

He took out his wallet and removed the tightly wadded bills.

"I have three hundred kroner. Give it to your landlady as a down payment. It will be a gift from me, not a loan." He handed her the money and she quickly stuffed the bills in her bra with no expression. She wiped the tears off her cheek with the edge of the napkin.

"Thank you. I will give you a massage by appointment. I will walk on your back and straighten you. That will cost only three hundred kroner. I will not accept a gift. I will not be indebted to you. I will excuse my debt by walking on your back."

She stood up and began to leave again.

"Leda, sit."

"I won't sit. Thank you for the money."

"You will wait. How will I get back without you steering the swan boat?"

"You will steer it yourself."

"Hold on. Sit down. Have some bread and potatoes."

"Danish potatoes. Kartofler. I don't eat this kartofler. I'm not hungry. Danes love kartofler. I do not eat them. They put weight on my hips. Here is my card. Jonny Levin, you are a decent man after all. I have to go back to the street now to search for the rest of the money. Ciao. You will call me or I will call you."

She dropped her card on his plate.

Leda Renauskas Vicivious
Masseuse and Physical Therapist
Shopping Service
Discounts at all stores
Private Studio
Model, Your Guide
Adventures

Tel. — 920758 - 4
20 Konigsgaard   Krulesfjord

"I'm going to the ladies' toilet to warm my hands on the hand dryer. It is freezing here. Ask my friend Petrius at the dock. He will help you with the swan boat. I will go on foot. Do not try to go on foot. You will never find your way. Petrius will help you with a good boat."

She bent over him and kissed him on the lips.

"Goodbye, Jonny Levin."

50

He watched her turn and walk through the crowd in the opposite direction and in a moment she was gone.

He shook his head and made a small sandwich of matjes herring, thin slices of potato with vinaigrette and onions on a square of rye bread. He took a sip of Aquavit and looked at her card.

He called for the check and left the waitress what he thought was a decent tip. Then he got up and walked through the crowd. The Aquavit had affected his legs and they felt slightly numb. He'd weakened and given in to her. She was quite an actress, but three hundred kroner, what was that—thirty dollars? It wouldn't be much help to her if she really was about to be evicted. What would Victor Borge have done if he'd been alive and faced with Leda? Would he have handed her his secret *pushkeh*? No, Borge was too shrewd. He'd become an American millionaire. A chicken farmer somewhere on the East Coast. A purveyor of packaged chicken. Borge would have been too smart to have become involved with her. He should have given her more than thirty dollars. He could have asked her to meet him later at the hotel and cashed a traveler's check for her and really helped her. Still he knew she wasn't telling him the truth. He had her card, though. He could call on her, look her studio over and see if she really was a masseuse. He could make an assessment of her situation. He'd be like an appraiser. He felt a real attraction for this young woman. Her hair had a lovely fragrance. It was still in his nostrils as he wandered down to the dock and looked for her friend Petrius.

Petrius was at the end of the dock in a blue striped T-shirt and a white Danish flat sailor's cap with a black ribbon embossed in gold with the name of a Danish ship. He seemed to be in his early twenties. Petrius held the swan boat steady for him while he got in and sat down. Then he showed him the steering wheel, the throttle lever, the klaxon and turned on the motor and running

51

lights. He pointed in the direction of the main Tivoli pier and shoved the boat with his foot out into the channel and gestured to accelerate by pulling down the lever. The swan boat quickly began to move away from the pier and in a moment he was alone navigating toward the lights of the Tivoli dock.

He looked up at the stars and there were his old friends Castor and Pollux. He would just hold the nape of the swan's graceful carved prow between the two constellations.

Maybe Victor Borge would have given her the entire four thousand kroner. But Borge was a cautious gentleman, an elegant man who could charm an audience in a hundred ways. Borge wouldn't have let himself become enchanted by Leda. He had too much self-control. But Borge was dead and he felt very much alive steering by the polarity of Castor and Pollux, adrift in the swan boat channel, moving through the colored lights reflected on the channel.

He tried to imitate a few of Borge's famous tongue clicks. Borge would have just pushed his piano bench back and given her a few clicks of his tongue and shaken his head in commiseration and given her nothing. No *rachmones* from Borge. Although tongue clicks were probably the earliest form of communicating sorrow.

Still she was really a beautiful young woman. He could still feel her lips pressed against his neck and the touch of her breasts on his back. She made him think of Robert Herrick's poem about "Julia" although Herrick wasn't steering a swan boat when he wrote it.

He looked up again at Castor and Pollux and kept his hand on the tiller, cleared his throat, and began reciting Herrick's poem quietly to himself.

UPON JULIA'S CLOTHES -

Wheneas in silks my Julia goes,
Then, then, methinks, how sweetly flows
The liquefaction of her clothes!

Next, when I cast mine eyes and see
That brave vibration each way free,
— O how that glittering taketh me!

He pulled into the swan boat pier rather easily, touching with just a little bump. He handed the hawser to another young man in white trousers and a straw Venetian gondolier's hat. The Danes were good with hats. He'd have to learn to interchange hats. He could be a different person with each hat. He could be a sea captain, a lover, a gambler, or a money lender. If he'd given her four thousand kroner he could be a Danish shylock and wear a little red Venetian yarmulke, "Hath not a Jew blood? Doth not a Jew bleed?" Something like that from "The Merchant of Venice". He should have given her the money and taken her cross as collateral.

6

THERE WAS THE CONSTANT SOUND of the screaming of the riders on a huge lighted Twirl-A-Wheel. Round and round they were flung, screaming. Beyond the trees ahead he heard the piping of the carousel and walked over a little hill and there was Mooney

53

Levine standing alone and slowly twirling on the edge of the carousel.

"Hi there Professor, I'm just giving this a test. I want to see if it's working right."

He watched Mooney slowly whirl by on the platform while the calliope played a Strauss Waltz, what was it, 'The Merry Widow'? That wasn't Strauss that was Lehar.

The platform slowed and Mooney stepped off and the carousel came to a stop. He was in his brown Italian sports jacket and was wearing a yellow silk tie and the same initialed blue shirt with the white round tab collar and the ML crest on the pocket and one cuff.

"How do you like my stallions? I have to do a little cosmetic job on a few."

"Hold this Professor." He handed Jonny a leather case that had tiny bottles of paint and brushes.

"Now, look at this lion's mouth. I'll take the red paint and just barely outline the lips. They're not right. They should snarl. If you do the lips with just another touch of red they'll look ferocious. Scare the crap out of the kids."

He held the brush between his teeth and carefully traced a thin red line around the lion's mouth that he curled into a snarl. Just as quickly he took a tiny pointed brush from the case and edged the red line with a thin black line. "There, now they look like they could bite your *toches* off."

"See that rose on that chariot over there? Its petals are broken. Some kid probably kicked them off. I've got a tube of plastic wood." He took it out of the case and reformed a perfect set of rose petals, rounding them with his index finger.

"Now the eyes of some of the stallions. Take a walk with me around the platform and look at the eyes. Look for the eyes that don't gleam. It's got to be like magic for the kids. The horses gotta invite you to climb up on them. There's one. Look at its eyes. They've gone dead."

He took another brush and tube and quickly touched the pupils of the horse's eyes.

"I got another joke for you Professor," he said while he worked on the eyes.

"Big black Cadillac pulls up to the entrance of one of the Miami hotels. Like the Americana, the Eden Roc, the Saxony. A little old Jewish lady is helped out by her chauffeur. Her girlfriend who lives at the hotel is standing there to meet her.

"'Where's your grandson, Rose? I thought you were bringing him,' the girlfriend says.

"'Wait a minute.' The old lady points at her chauffeur and he wraps the grandson, an eleven year old boy, in a blanket and carries him into the hotel.

"The girlfriend says, 'you didn't tell me he can't walk.'

"'He can walk – but thank God he doesn't have to.'

"You've got to laugh at that one, Jonny – 'He can walk – but thank God he don't have to' – so there, how do you like those eyes? Don't they look like evil eyes? You've gotta scare the crap out of the ladies, too, not just the kids."

"Okay, Professor, I've got another one for you – little old Jewish lady goes to her travel agent and insists on buying a ticket to Tibet.

"'Tibet, Mrs. Goldstein? At your age? Why Tibet?' the travel agent asks her.

"'I want to go, that's all. It's none of your business why. Just book the ticket.'

"'Okay, so I won't ask. Such a big journey. I won't ask any more questions.' She books a round trip ticket to Katmandu.

"A week later Mrs. Goldstein arrives in Tibet and is met by a guide. 'Where do you want to go madam?' he asks her.

"I want to see the Dalai Lama.'

"'I don't think so. That isn't possible.'

"'I want to see the Dalai Lama.'

"'I don't think that can be arranged madam.'

"'You just tell him that Mrs. Goldstein is here from Newark to see him.'

"She goes back to the hotel and goes to sleep. In the morning, to the amazement of the guide, an official car is sent for her and she's taken to the top of the mountain to the palace where she's ushered in, but stopped by the palace guard.

"'I want to see the Dalai Lama,' she tells him.

"'And who shall I tell His Eminence are you?'

"'Tell him Mrs. Goldstein from Newark.'

"Much to his surprise, the guard is told by the Dalai Lama's aide to bring her in immediately.

"So she's shown down the long red carpet leading to a dais. There, sitting on a platform covered with flowers, is a short bald man with glasses peering at her over his bifocals. You can see by his expression that there's a hint of recognition.

"The aide steps forward, a gold bell is rung.

"'Madam, you may address the Dalai Lama.'

"Mrs. Goldstein stands before him, clears her throat, purses her lips and waggles her finger.

"'Elliott,' she says, 'All right already, your father wants you to come home.'"

Mooney Levine shakes with laughter. "'All right already, Elliott, your father wants you to come home."

"Do you get it Jonny? Her son Elliott is the Dalai Lama."

"How's that, is that a good one? First—'He can walk, but thank God he don't have to.' Now—'Elliott, come home al-

56

ready.' Now it's your turn Jonny. You got any good ones? I need some good jokes. I collect them at home and I send them out by email to my friends and my customers."

"No, I don't think I know a joke. Not one."

"Not one?"

"I can't think of one."

"Not one Jewish joke?"

"I can't think of one."

"Some Professor you are. You can't tell me a Jewish joke. If you tell me one I'll tell you the one place in Copenhagen you can buy a piece of halvah."

"I don't eat halvah."

"There's only one Jewish deli in Copenhagen. It's right near our hotel. Everyone eats halvah. Even Arafat loved halvah. What do you think the first thing he asked for when they took him to the hospital in Paris from his headquarters in Ramallah? He asked for some halvah."

"Okay, I got one for you Mooney. I just remembered it. Myron Cohen's favorite joke."

"I love Myron Cohen. What is it, the one about the lady on the plane and her diamond ring that she shows to the Texan sitting next to her?"

"No this is Myron Cohen's most famous joke – 'Lady is home in bed with her lover. They're both middle aged and having this affair once a week on Thursday afternoons. But this Thursday, the husband unexpectedly comes home. They hear the front door open. They're up in the master bedroom. The man who's the lover, he's a little guy, jumps out of bed, grabs his clothes and shoes and hides in her closet. The wife pretends she's asleep.

"The husband comes upstairs into the bedroom and he senses something going on. He says to the wife, 'What's happening here?' – 'Nothing', she says. He sees the rumpled sheets and the bedspread thrown back.

"Who's here? There's someone here.'

"There's no one here.'

"Oh yeah?' He starts looking around, poking the bed-covers and looking around the bedroom. Suddenly he opens the closet door and there's the little man.

"The man looks up at the husband, shrugs and says, 'Everyone's gotta be somewhere.'"

Mooney laughs, "That's a great joke, Jonny. 'Everyone's gotta be somewhere.' That's a famous joke. I heard it already, but it's a great joke."

"Okay, one more for you Jonny and then I got to set up the brass ring machine and the calliope. Those two ladies from the hotel are coming here at eight and then we're all going to the séance as my guests. You're coming too. I've got three seats re-served in the front row."

"Here's my last joke Jonny. The famous diamond joke. A little Jewish lady on a plane to London seated next to a big Texan in a ten gallon hat. She's got a huge ring and the Texan taps her on the shoulder and says to her, 'Pardon me ma'am, but is that the Hope Diamond?' 'No,' she says to him, 'that's the Klopman diamond.' 'Well,' he says, 'it's just beautiful. Tell me ma'am, does that diamond have a curse on it like the Hope Diamond?' 'Yes it does,' she says. 'Tell me, what is the curse ma'am?' 'The curse? The curse is Mr. Klopman.'"

He slaps Jonny on the back. "You get it Jonny – 'The curse is Mr. Klopman.'"

"That's an old joke Mooney."

"You've heard it?"

"The Klopman diamond joke, I've heard it."

"Okay, I've got to set up the brass ring machine. You climb up on the neck of that giraffe and hold your hand out. I'll turn on the machine. There are only three or four brass ring machines left in the world. I've got one here and one on Coney Island. All the rings are silver except one is brass. When they come flying by you see if you can grab the brass ring. Silver don't count. You get nothing for silver, *bupkes*. Grab the brass ring, you get a free table setting for four of Royal Copenhagen. Each time I turn it on though, if you play, it costs you fifty kroner. You got the best chance leaning from the neck of the giraffe. You'll be closer than you are sitting on a stallion."

"I'm not going to get up on a giraffe." When he said the word "giraffe" a line of poetry from an author whose name he couldn't remember began to throb in his head... "Maculate Giraffe".

"Why not?"

"I'm leaving. You finish your work. I'll be back at eight to watch the ladies grab for the brass rings."

"Suit yourself, Jonny. But don't forget, I've got all of you booked for the séance. She's a great fortune teller, Josefina. There's no one like her. You'll be glad you came. If you've got any problems, she'll solve them for you."

"I don't have any problems."

"Everyone's got problems. Here, I'll give you another little spritz." Mooney took out his abalone shell spritzer and gave Jonny a spritz of pheromone. "I call it "Danish Delight." The Danish girls go nuts for it. It worked for me, has it worked for you?"

"Mooney, no more spritzing. I don't want more."

"Just another tiny little spritz. It only lasts for maybe an hour or two burchik. Men our age need some extra allure." He sprayed Jonny's lapels. "I just put it lightly on your lapels. It seems to work best when it's absorbed on your clothes. I gave you just a touch. A scent like a woman's musk perfume. Do you remember the ads for Tabu? Are you old enough Jonny to remember Tabu? The girls in my high school in the Bronx all wore Tabu. They used to drive me crazy. Beautiful young Jewish girls soaked in Tabu with pearls and cashmere sweaters no one could afford."

"I remember Tabu. The ad with the violinist with the lady in his arms. He's holding his violin and kissing her over the piano."

"That's how my stuff works. It even works on American ladies. Those two from the hotel. The thin one goes for you Jonny. I can tell. The fat one's not my type. But the thin one, she's got a nice body. A couple of rich broads from Chicago. I like the young blonde Danish ladies, like the two desk clerks. They're my type."

"They seem to go for you Mooney. They give you special flowers."

"I told both of them to meet me later tonight at the Radisson SAS at the casino. I said I'd back them at roulette. Why don't you come along? I can't handle two of them. They said they might show."

"No, I'll come to the séance, but not to the casino."

"Okay, Jonny, suit yourself." He stuck his hand out and touched his knuckles to Jonny's. "Eight o'clock. Listen to what Josefina has to say. Your luck will change."

He walked away from Mooney to a carnival booth where darts were thrown at yellow balloons tied to a wall. Three darts for ten kroner, a dollar. If you broke three balloons you got your pick of cheap prizes. He bought three darts and aimed and tossed one and broke a yellow balloon. He tossed a second dart and broke another yellow balloon. He aimed carefully on the third try and hit the balloon, but the dart bounced off obliquely. The man who ran the booth shrugged, but then smiled and handed him a fourth dart and pointed at the balloons. Another chance for free. He carefully aimed the dart, threw it and the balloon popped. "*Tak*," he said. The man pointed to the prizes and picked one out for him. It was a framed photo of Queen Margrethe as a young woman. Just his kind of prize. "*Tak*," he said again. Then he mumbled, "Thank you."

Now he had a framed photograph of Queen Margrethe as a beautiful young woman. It would go with his prize from the shooting booth, a Danish flag pin. He'd forgotten to wear the Danish flag pin tonight. Mooney Levine was very annoying. He didn't want to be spritzed with pheromones. The whole incident on the swan boat seemed almost unreal, phantasmagoric. A word right out of Poe. It never happened. There never was a young woman named Leda who put her arms around him. It never happened. He had too much dignity to have allowed it to happen. Still, there was her lingering fragrance. That was real.

The next booth was a shooting booth of sorts, only the guns were water guns. You aimed a stream of water flowing from a mounted water machine gun at metal bullseye flanges. If you hit the bullseye flange in the center it caused a wooden rabbit to advance up a tube above the targets. A race of wooden rabbits and the first rabbit to climb to the finish line took home a prize. Better than a race of "Maculate Giraffes." Why maculate? Maybe because they eat the leaves off tree tops. He bought a ten kroner token and sat down at his machine gun with a seated group of Danes all waiting for a buzzer to sound. He toggled the gun so the sight was squarely on the bullseye. The buzzer rang. Little girls shrieked behind their fathers. The bullseye flange swayed as the water hit it, but he kept a steady stream of water on it. The buzzer rang again. His rabbit won the race. He chose a small teddy bear and walked away again a winner.

61

Two wins in a row. Maybe Mooney was right. His luck would change. What was the name of the tall slender woman from Chicago? Elyse Friedberg? Attractive and confident with slender long legs. He had a choice. He could walk back to the hotel, lock himself in his room and work on his novel. Maybe stop on the way and visit Andersen and give him a little shry. Something more than his last glottal eech. Maybe a real Bellowian shry. He could touch knuckles with Andersen in the moonlight then go back to the room, close the door and write. Or he could return to the carousel and see if Elyse Friedberg would show. He just didn't feel like sitting alone in his room with his teddy bear and framed photo of Queen Margrethe or further constructing the cemetery. The night was too beautiful to sit alone in the room.

He turned back toward the carousel. He'd read somewhere that Queen Margrethe was a chain smoker. She was still lovely though, in her fifties, in her newspaper photos. Now he had a plastic sack with her framed photograph and a teddy bear. He'd easily out shot the Danish fathers. As the young shooting booth attendant had told him, Americans are very good with guns. He'd stop by her booth again, perhaps after the séance, and see if he could win a Royal Guardsman, the tiny wooden statue of the blue, waistcoated royal guardsman with the bearskin shako. Then he'd have a trio, the chain smoking beautiful queen, her shako-topped guardsman and the Danish flag pin. All because of his prowess as an American marksman.

He turned and walked back over the tiny rise to the carousel. It was exactly eight o'clock. *Klokken 8* as the Danes say. The two American women were standing there, both looking at their watches as he approached. They wore black slack suits and black cashmere sweaters with long bright colored silk floral scarves. Elyse Friedberg smiled brightly as she saw him.

62

"You came. I'm so pleased."

"Yes, I'm ready to be séanced."

"You remember Martha?"

"Hello Professor," Martha said to him. "We met at breakfast."

"Yes, I remember. Please call me John. J-O-H-N. John Levin." He'd be John with these American women.

"Where did you say you taught, John?"

"I didn't say."

"Martha, stop it. You promised me you weren't going to do that. Don't start."

"I don't see why he won't tell us where he teaches. If he lives in Evanston I already know where he teaches. What's the big secret?"

He answered her, "The secret is that there is no secret. It's sort of a Zen secret."

Mooney Levine hopped off the carousel and greeted them. He put his arm around Martha Selig.

"Hello sweetheart. Glad to see you ladies. Hi, professor. Okay, just get on any one of these animals. The lion, the giraffe, the stallions. I'll turn on the brass ring machine. There are only a few in the world. I have two. One here and one at Coney. Get up there before all those Danish mamas grab the best seats for their kids. I'll let you on free. You're all my guests. When the rings come flying by, see if you can grab the brass ring. There's only one. If you get it you win a place setting for four of Royal Copenhagen. Whoever sits on the giraffe has the best chance."

"That's me," Martha Selig said. "I want the giraffe."

"You got it Martha."

She stepped up on the platform. She was a big woman with a large behind and as Mooney helped her up on the giraffe he pinched her.

"My god, Elyse."

63

LOWELL B. KOMIE

"What?"

"Be careful of that man, did you see him pinch me?"

"No."

"Get on, Elyse. Get on the lion behind me."

Elyse Friedberg swung herself easily on the lion. "Okay John, you get on. How about a lion next to me."

"I think I'll watch."

"No, no, that's not fair. Climb on the lion."

He got up on the lion and Mooney rang a bell and all the Danish children came running with their parents and climbed up on the animals. Some of the children were as young as two and were hoisted up. The fathers and mothers stood behind them. A few adults got on the stallions. Some rode in the chariots.

The calliope music began softly.

Mooney Levine was talking through a loudspeaker in English. His remarks were immediately translated into Danish after each sentence by a smiling young Danish teenage girl with a large yellow flower at her throat.

"Ladies and gentlemen, boys and girls, you are about to ride on one of the world's most famous carousels."

"The Tivoli carousel has 36 jumping horses – fourteen standing horses – they're all stallions. They're all hand-carved by the greatest wooden carousel carvers on earth from Brooklyn, New York. Notice the roses woven into their manes and the baby-faced angels on their flanks."

"We also have two wooden chariots, carved by the same carvers. Please don't let your children kick the wooden rose petals or the angels on the chariots and horses. We know kids get excited, but don't let them kick the rose petals and angels.

"All the animals and chariots are very safe. We don't go at high speeds. We twirl slowly and you'll all have a chance at the brass ring machine.

64

"We have a sixty-six key Gebruder organ. The Copenhagen organ is even larger than our Coney Island organ and plays only waltzes and love songs. It's like being at a concert at the Royal Opera House.

"We have one of the world's only brass ring machines. When the music starts, silver rings will come flying by you. One of them, though, isn't silver, it's made of brass. Grab at the rings and try to find it. Each ring you take will cost you fifty kroner. If you grab the brass ring you'll win a beautiful china table setting for four from Royal Copenhagen—no children can play though. Only adults can reach for the rings. Remember, if you take one it will cost you fifty kroner and we'll collect when you get off.

"All right, is everyone ready? I'll start the Gebruder. See if you recognize the song. It's a very famous waltz. A Viennese waltz, a gift from Vienna to Copenhagen. Hold your children. Keep them firmly on their mounts. Have a good time. Adults only for the rings – okay – here we go – the "Merry Widow" waltz."

The organ began to play the waltz from the "Merry Widow" and the carousel began to slowly turn.

The children were frozen into silence when the carousel began to move. The younger ones sat very solemnly holding onto the brass poles with their parents alongside reassuring them. The older children quickly grew bored until the stallions began to move up and down and the children would post in the stirrups and point to each other and laugh. Then the rings began to descend, slowly at first then twirling and flashing tantalizingly as they whirled by just out of reach of the adults.

Mooney Levine's voice again came over the loudspeaker.

"Ladies and gentlemen, the rings have descended. As they fly by you, see if you can find the brass ring."

The young Danish woman with the yellow flower at her

throat translated as Mooney paused and gazed at her with fatherly affection. She looked like a young, virginal, Danish Marilyn Monroe.

"Remember, there's only one brass ring, so look them over carefully before you pick one."

"They all look alike to me," Elyse said to Martha.

"No Elyse, I see it. That one there. It's coming around now." Martha pointed.

Some of the Danish men had reached up and plucked silver rings over the necks of their horses.

Suddenly Martha threw herself over the neck of the giraffe and lunged at what looked like a tiny comet whirring and flashing gold in the glistening circle of silver rings. "I got it," she screamed, and lunged over the neck of the giraffe falling to the floor of the carousel clutching the brass ring and twisting in agony.

"Oh my God Elyse, my rotor cuff. I tore it." She lay writhing on the floor as the carousel kept whirling and the Gebruder played on. She had the brass ring clutched in her hands.

"I tore my rotor cuff, Elyse. I can feel the tear. I've done it before. I can't move my right arm. Call an ambulance. Get me out of here."

Elyse bent over her.

"Martha are you okay?"

"No I'm not okay. I tore my rotor cuff. I could feel it rip. I'm in God-awful pain. I'm going to sue that man. Call an ambulance."

"Do you want to go to the hospital?"

"No hospital, just back to the hotel. This has happened to me before. A few days' rest and I'll be okay, but I'm going to sue. That giraffe's neck was so slippery and covered with some kind of grease to make it slippery, like a greased pig."

"A greased giraffe?"

"Go look at it and feel it yourself."

Mooney Levine and his young Danish assistant bent over Martha and helped her to her feet. Mooney took her long scarf and made a sling out of it and walked her over to one of the chariots and sat her down. He tried to soothe her.

"Martha, it was just an accident. People get excited and fall off the mounts as they reach for the rings. It happens all the time. There's no grease on the giraffe's neck. I'd have to be crazy to do something like that. We have a perfect safety record." He flashed the reflective light from his glass ring at two passing Tivoli guards and the guards came running over and stood next to him beside the chariot. They looked like large duplicates of the carved wooden guard figures on the carousel.

"Martha, these men will escort you to Royal Copenhagen. You can turn the brass ring over to them and they'll wait with you while you claim your prize and then they'll take you back to the hotel. Now just let me feel your shoulder for a minute." He pretended to adjust her sling, but instead with just a quick movement of his fingers manipulated her shoulder back into place.

"What are you doing to me?"

"Just relax Martha, you'll be okay."

"You're hurting me."

"Only for a second. Now try moving your arm." He untied her sling.

"You're going to be okay Martha."

"Elyse, look, I can move my arm."

"So go pick up your prize Martha." Mooney gave her a little pat on the behind. "And here's a flower from me." He plucked the yellow flower from his assistant's throat and fastened the wire stem around the zipper of Martha's sweater.

"I have to go with her John," Elyse began to follow Martha and the two guardsmen. Then she turned back, "I can't go to the séance John, but call our room when you get back to the hotel." She said the hotel room number into his ear, "502". Her lips seemed to linger at his ear. "502," she said again. "Call me and I'll come down and we'll have a drink in the bar. Believe me, I'll need one."

They watched Martha being ushered away by the tall Tivoli guards.

"She'll be okay Jonny. I clicked her shoulder back into place. What a *klutz*."

"Did you really grease the giraffe's neck?"

"Just a little."

"What do you mean, 'just a little'?"

"I always put a thin film of neats foot oil on the giraffe's neck. If I didn't I'd have a winner every time. It's too easy to grab the brass ring from the giraffe's neck so I grease up the giraffe a little."

"What about at Coney Island?"

"No I never grease the giraffe up at Coney. I could get my throat cut at Coney if I got caught. But I don't give away such fancy prizes at Coney. No Royal Copenhagen. Sometimes I give away cheap china and silverware, but most often big plush dolls for the girlfriends."

Jonny thought about changing the phrase 'Maculate Giraffe' to 'Greased Giraffe' but he didn't feel any poetic sense from the change. The phrase would lose its symmetry. Maybe 'Maculate Giraffe' was a line of T.S. Eliot or perhaps a line of Auden's.

"Jonny, we'll walk over to the séance together, we're already late, but before we leave I've got one more joke for you. Just a short one." A young Danish man in an open guardsman's tunic and a Danish captain's hat gave Mooney a two-fingered salute and Mooney tossed his ring of keys for the carousel to him. "Okay, Jonny, listen to this one."

"Two Jewish men are walking past a Catholic church and as they pass they see a sign, 'Come in and convert. You'll be paid ten dollars'.

"'I think I'll go in for a minute,' one man says. 'Wait for me here.'

"The friend waits outside the church for maybe ten minutes and finally the man comes out.

"Well, did you convert?" he asked his friend.

"Yes I did."

"Did they pay you the ten dollars?"

"The friend looked at him. 'You people. All you think about is money.'"

"How do you like that one, Jonny? 'You people. All you think about is money.' Is that a keeper?"

He was still lost in exploring the parallelism of 'Maculate Giraffe' and 'Greased Giraffe' when suddenly a joke of his own popped into his head like an email popup. "Did you hear about Philip Roth's new book?" he could ask Mooney – "No," he'd answer. "What's it called?" – "The Grapes of Roth." Not bad he told himself, but Mooney wouldn't know who Philip Roth was so he didn't tell him, but that was fairly clever, "The Grapes of Roth". Maybe it could fit somewhere into his novel. He could put it on one of the little grave markers.

"Mine eyes have seen the glory of the coming of the Lord.

"He is trampling out the vintage where the Grapes of Roth are stored."

That would be good for a grave marker with a tiny grey dove perched on top and peeking over the side. Or maybe two grey doves. Kaene Philip Roth. He wrote his guts out trying to win the Nobel Prize and look what it did for him. He's made millions. But Bellow, that dessicated cocksman with the beautiful young wife, and Singer, that crafty old cocksman and son of a rabbi, who picked out his stories and novels in *mameloshen* on an old Yiddish typewriter, they each got the Nobel—and Roth, he got *bupkes, gornisht*—but he's still locking himself in his room all night writing, hoping for a Nobel. You call that a life?

7

THE SÉANCE WAS HELD in a tent lit only by candlelight. There were about eight people seated in a circle around a large wooden table. Mooney led him to a card table, then Mooney disappeared behind a curtain. There were orange shadows of figures enlarged by the candlelight dancing on the walls of the tent. A scratchy record of a wailing Arab song of flutes and oboes began and an aroma of Middle Eastern fragrances wafted over the audience. A young woman dancer in veils, barefoot, her face hidden in the darkness, appeared and whirled and whirled around the room and clicked golden castanets as she turned and suddenly she also disappeared. Mooney's voice came from a microphone behind a curtain.

"Ladies and gentlemen, welcome. In a minute you will meet Madame Josefina who has just come to Copenhagen from her home in Jerusalem for this one time appearance for M. Levine International Productions. As you'll see, Madame Josefina is a talent of great magical powers. She can solve your problems in a New York minute. She can help you if you'll let her work her magic on you. Madame Josefina is an international sorceress, but even international sorceresses have to make a living. So remember, the first question to the Madame tonight is absolutely free. After that each question will be one-hundred kroner or ten dollars paid in advance to be collected by my assistant before the question is

70

asked. Any questions will be put to the Madame in a private booth over there." Mooney flashed his ring and a beam of light, like a laser pointer, illuminated a ragged looking carnival booth that looked like a frayed cabana or an ancient canvas confessional.

"But before taking any private questions, Madame Josefina will conduct the séance you have all been waiting for." Suddenly the reedy music swelled into a crescendo – "Now here she is, direct from the ancient walls of Jerusalem. Welcome her to the beautiful towers of Tivoli Park Copenhagen—the International Seer and Sorceress, Madame Josefina. Give her a nice hand ladies and gentlemen. Give her a real Danish welcome."

A little old lady that looked as wrinkled and furtive as Mother Theresa dressed in the same kind of saffron robe limped out on the stage and sat down holding her cane and blinking at the audience.

"Vhy haf I come to Copenhagen?" she said in a heavy Polish/Yiddish accent. "God only knows. So cold here and the wrong kind of herring. No schmaltz herring. Vot kind of town with only von delicatessen and only chopped herring and matjes herring, but no schmaltz herring?"

She shook her head sadly. "But for Mister Levine I fly, but only for two nights I vill hold the séances. Already I feel pain in my heart. I need some special water with bubbles like *grepsvasser* to take my nitro pill. So he's my friend and he gets me my special water which, by the way, they don't have on SAS. SAS, such a name. It was to me like SS only with an extra A. SS, the Gestapo, who killed my beloved Bruno Schulz in Drohobycz in Poland. Who vas Bruno Schulz? He vas my fiancé. A great Jewish-Polish writer and artist. We hoped to marry, but the Gestapo killed him and left me alone. Only do I haf memories. Only painful memories of one of the greatest writers and artists in the western world. He vas the Polish Kafka, Bruno Schulz.

"But I come here to honor another great writer and artist, a Dane not a *landsman*, but a maker of fairy tales. Who is dot man whose statue is standing in the moonlight right outside the walls of Tivoli vit his top hat, a book on his knee, and his cane? Dot man with the top hat and cane is the great Danish writer Hans Christian Andersen. The spinner of fairy tales, which kind the world has not known since. 'The Ugly Duckling,' the von about a mermaid, 'The Little Mermaid,' the von about the match girl, 'The Little Match Girl,' not even a Yiddish writer could spin out such magic fairy tales like Hans Christian Andersen. No one – Anski, poof – he writes only about Hassids. No Hassids in Denmark. Zeitlin, poof – Julian Tuwim, that imposter, that fancy man who moved from Warsaw to New York, piff-poff. Not even my beloved Bruno could write about 'The Little Match Girl.' I vas Bruno's Little Match Girl, me Josefina. The little match girl of Bruno Schulz. He was engaged to another Josefina, a Catholisher Josefina Czelinska before me. But he dumped her and promised me the marriage. I am the real Josefina, Josefina Goldstyne, the Jewish Josefina, the love of Bruno Schulz's life.

"So for the Danes who saved their Jews from the Nazis, the only ones in all Europe brave enough to do so, I come to Copenhagen to honor their great writer, Hans Christian Andersen. With this séance, I will put him back in touch with Jenny Lind, his love. I will bring them back together. As I, Josefina Goldstyne, was loved by Bruno Schulz, Hans Christian Andersen was in love with the great soprano, the Swedish Nightingale,with a voice like an angel, Jenny Lind.

"Tonight I vill restore their love and bring them back together."

Suddenly a curtain was dropped and Madame Josefina was gone. More incense wafted into the tent. The reedy music began again, but then the record was pulled with a screech and the beautiful soprano voice of the Swedish soprano Jenny Lind began flowing into the tent and suddenly Jenny Lind, appeared in shadow behind the curtain.

The tones were dulcet, smooth, and ripe but the shadowy figure of Jenny Lind looked vaguely familiar to him even in the sparse light of the candles. She turned and came out from behind the curtain and faced the audience. He recognized her. She was Mooney's assistant, the virginal, apple-cheeked Danish Marilyn Monroe. She was both the veiled dancer whirling with the golden castanets and the Swedish Nightingale, Jenny Lind. Madame Josefina came back on stage.

"Und now Jenny Lind will sing for us her famous aria, 'Svenska Flicka' vhich means a young Swedish girl in love. She vill sing this aria, not only for your ears, but also for the ears of Hans Christian Andersen who, by the vay if you've ever seen his picture, had big ears like an elephant and a big nose, a schnozz so big he had a very hard time getting women to fall in love with him. He vas, in fact, the original Ugly Duckling, that face, vot a *punim*, but vot a magnificent heart. It was in his heart that he was such a great lover.

"Now vhile Jenny Lind sings her sweet aria, please all of you in the first row put your hands down flat on the table and vhen I tell you to knock on the table – you knock. If we hear someone knocking back, ve will know then that it's him, Mr. Andersen, the Ugly Duckling. So silence – absolute silence while Jenny sings her love song. The sad song of a young Swedish girl looking for her lover. Und by the vay, did the Little Mermaid ever find her lover? Who knows the answer? Did she ever find the prince – of course she did, but vhat price did she pay? Vot did she haf to give up to meet her love? Vot did the wicked witch of the underwater kingdom do to her before she fed the mermaid the magic potion to change her fins to legs and bring her up from the sea – she took her tongue. She cut out her tongue – so all you ladies who vant to be mermaids and rise from the sea – best to keep your mouths shut.

"Okay, in America they play this game—Knock, Knock.

"I say Knock, knock.

"You say who's there?"

There suddenly was a knocking on the table—knock, knock.

Jenny Lind kept singing, but now she began whirling and whirling as she sang.

"Who's dere? Who's dat knocking?"

"Isak," a tortured raspy voice answered.

"Isak who? Isak Bashevis Singer, the Yiddish writer who wrote 'Yentl'? You call that a fairy tale? A girl who dresses as a boy and tries to win the love of a yeshiva *bocher*. Dot Bashevis stole from 'Yidl Mitn Fidl,' the same story. A girl with her violin disguised as a boy wit Polish violinists on the road falls in love. Bashevis just stole Yidl and made her into Yentl but still no fairy tale like 'The Little Mermaid'. Nowhere near as good.

"Is that really you Bashevis? The boy who wit his brother Israel Joshua used to climb the trees in Swider by the seaside and sit up in the trees and try to write fairy tales?"

"It is not Bashevis," again the croaking voice.

"Well then who? Isak who?"

"Isak Dinesen."

"Isak Dinesen, the famous Danish woman writer, the Baroness Blixen? So vot message do you bring to us tonight, Baroness?"

" – All of you keep your hands on the table – vait for the knocking."

" – Knock, knock."

"Vot is the message?"

"The message is – 'I had a farm in Afrika'."

"Oy, ve all know that message. Tell me Isak Dinesen, haf you seen Hans Christian Andersen? Can you bring him to the table tonight? Knock three times if you can."

Again, the raspy, tortured voice.

"I have not seen him."

"Who? Who have you not seen?"

"Hans Christian Andersen."

"Vhere is Hans Christian Andersen. Do you know where he is, Baroness? All of you. Keep your hands down on the table."

"Denys Finch-Hatton. Where is he?"

"Vot about Denys Finch-Hatton?"

"He flew away from me."

"Ve all know about Finch-Hatton. He was your lover in 'Out of Africa' and he got in his plane and flew away like a bird and never came back. Only he crashed into a mountain. Den you buried him up on that hill where the lions came and laid down on his grave. I remember dot scene. But Finch-Hatton ve don't look for, ve vant only Hans Christian Andersen."

"I want Denys Finch-Hatton."

"Ve know all that already. But we vant 'The Ugly Duckling'. The man wit the big schnozz who wrote 'The Little Mermaid'. Haf you seen him?"

"I see him quite often. He comes to visit me at my grave in Elsinore. Always by moonlight. In his top hat and with his cane. We talk Danish together in the moonlight."

"Vot do you talk about?"

"I ask him if he has seen Denys."

"Vot does he say?"

"He says, 'no. never.' Then he tips his hat and walks away down the path. But always he turns and with his hat over his heart he asks me, if I have seen Jenny Lind?"

"His great love. Jenny Lind, the 'Swedish Nightingale'?"

"Yes."

75

"And vot do you say to him?"

"No, I have never seen her. I don't know where she is."

"I know vhere she is Isak."

"Where?"

"If I tell you vhere is Jenny Lind, vill you bring Hans Christian back with you to meet her?"

"Oh yes."

"She is here with us tonight."

"In this tent?"

"Yes, we vill show you – now all of you lift your hands from the table."

As everyone raised their hands the music began again and Jenny Lind appeared singing in her beautiful, sweet voice, slowly whirling around the table, her veils swirling.

"Do you hear her Isak?"

"The voice. It is so beautiful."

"It is Jenny Lind. She is vaiting here for Hans Christian. Bring him to us tomorrow night. Bring him. If you bring him to us I promise ve vill look for Finch-Hatton. I think I know vhere he is."

"You do?"

"I might."

"I will give you anything, anything, if you find him."

"Good night Isak Dinesen. I am growing weary. My powers are leaving me. I cannot see you anymore. Please, please all of you keep your hands on the table. Say goodbye to Isak Dinesen. Ve vill see you tomorrow night at eight. Same place, same time, same table. Good night Isak Dinesen, the Baroness Blixen."

The music began again. The reedy, atonal music. Jenny Lind came whirling out on the stage, only this time she was dressed again as a harem girl and she held a very frightened white chicken in a bamboo cage.

76

"Okay, now if any of you vant a private session with me, I vill see you in one of the booths over there."

Madame Josefina limped off the stage as the audience applauded and the harem girl bowed and twirled once and followed her with the white chicken in the bamboo cage.

Jonny Levin was the first to follow her to the tent for a personal consultation. He was the first in line.

The tent panel opened after a few minutes and the young Danish harem dancer beckoned him inside.

Madame Josefina was seated behind a small table with one foot propped up on a tufted cushion. She was holding a bottle of water.

"Oy, I could *plotz*. Vot a job this is. Dat Isak Dinesen. Did you see her *punim*? As ugly as Hans Christian Andersen. She looked like a dried prune. Uglier than Hans Christian. So, I'm supposed to find her true love vot flew away from her up into the sky in Africa? Dots vhat she wants from me? She buried him already with the lions on a hill, I'm supposed to find him? Vot a pair of *mashuggeners*. Her and her lover boy. She was vot? A baroness or something? Plenty it should cost her if I bring her Finch-Hatton back from the lions."

Madame Josefina took a drink of her special water.

"Thanks be to God for this *greppsvasser*." She gave a little belch. "Dot Mister Mooney Levine is a real *mensch*, he got for me a case of my special vater. Now with my bad leg, throbbing with sciatica, up on the cushion he got for me, already I feel better. My powers are coming back to me. So vot can I do for you young man?"

The Danish harem maiden stood at her side in the candlelight, her gaze falling on Jonny Levin, her nose twitching already at the scent he gave off, mixed in the tent with the odor of the chicken and the yellow tallow melting from the candle.

"Let me see your hand, mister. Give it over here to me."

Madame Josefina motioned to him to come closer.

"But first you give one-hundred kroner to Jenny Lind here."

He handed a hundred kroner bill to Jenny Lind and Madame Josefina snatched the bill away and held it over the candle. She squinted at the watermark, the shadowy profile of a young Queen Margrethe embedded in the bank note. She folded the bill and dropped it inside her toga.

"Gif to me your hand."

He put his hand in hers.

"Vot do you vant to know from me? Two questions. Two questions only."

She snapped her fingers at Jenny Lind and the handmaiden took the chicken out of its slotted cage and held it up to her breast.

"All right, go ahead and ask – question number 1."

"Madame Josefina, I've come to Denmark to write a novel. I'm a writer. Will I be able to write it? Can you help me?"

Her hooded eyes stared at him. "A writer? Every *putz* thinks he's a writer. Sit down in dot chair," she pointed to a stool. "Sit there. You vant to be a writer? Look vot happened to my darling Bruno Schulz. Dot fake, Cynthia Ozick, wrote about him in her 'The Messiah of Stockholm'. He never wrote such a novel vot name vas 'The Messiah' like Ozick said. There was no such book. I ought to know. I was with him every night in Drohobycz. Never was he writing on a novel. Day and night he was teaching carpentry to Polish kids in the high school. Teaching them to make birdhouses, chairs and tables. So now you say to me you vant to write a novel. Okay mister. Jenny Lind will hold dot white chicken over your head. *Shlogn Kapores* we call it. You know vot is *Shlogn Kapores*? On the night before Yom Kippur, a chicken is held over the head and your sins are transferred to the chicken and then its throat is slit and ve give it to the poorhouse. *Shlogn Kapores.* You vant this chicken's throat slit so you can become a writer? It's dot important to you dat you vant us to kill this poor chicken? No way. Ve don't slit our chicken's throat. Ve only got one chicken, so go ahead, Jenny Lind, twirl the chicken."

Jenny Lind twirled the chicken upside down, slowly over Jonny Levin's head and covered him with a veil. He sensed her cheap adolescent orange blossom perfume. Its sickly sweet odor filled his nostrils. Then she plucked a white feather from the chicken and stuck it through his lapel.

"All right, now you got this white feather. Maybe you'll be a writer. Maybe you'll finish your novel. Maybe not? Only God and this chicken knows. The chicken can't talk. God can talk. Maybe he'll talk to you later. All right. So vhere is question #2?"

"Will I fall in love here in Denmark Madame Josefina? Will I find a woman here?"

"Let me look at your hand again."

She pulled his hand toward the candle and peered at it.

"Silky smooth. Never did any labor. Not a rough, working man's hand. No calluses. My Bruno had calluses from all the carpentry he made. The birdhouses, the rocking horses. He made me a magnificent dollhouse like a castle, vit a roof I could take off and tiny furniture in every room, even with a baby already in a cradle in our bedroom. It could have been our baby, like a tiny Jesus in a crèche. Only Jews don't believe in baby Jesus. Are you a Jewish man? A Yid? You got a yiddisher *punim*. I say even with a hand like yours, silky smooth, never done no work, you, if you're a Jewish man, will find love in Denmark. Hamlet, that schmuck, found love here. So vhy not a yiddisher boy, can't he find his Ophelia? Only not quite so suicidal and so young with rocks already in her pocket. Maybe a nice Jewish woman wit a fish tank and colored pebbles in her fish tank, not a suicidal *shiksa*."

She snapped her fingers and Jenny Lind again took the chicken from its cage and held the chicken upside down over his head. She leaned toward him and whirled the chicken over him and covered him with her veils and pressed her breasts against his face.

"Oh my God," he thought lost in the sickly sweet odor of orange blossoms, a high school girl's fragrance.

"Okay, that's enough. Next," Madame Josefina held up her bottle of *grepsvasser* and took another swallow. "You're through, mister." She pointed to the opening of the canvas flap. "Enough already. Two questions. One hundred kroner. *Gai gesunt.* Go in good health."

As he turned to leave, Jenny Lind plucked another white chicken feather for his other lapel and thrust it through the fabric.

Enough already. Enough of Madame Josefina and her perfumed assistant. He walked away from the tent, the cheap orange blossom perfume in his nostrils. "Stay away from suicidal *shikshas*," she told him. How about apple-cheeked Danish hand maidens dressed as Arab odalisques? Enough already of séances and odalisques. He wouldn't stop at the shooting booth tonight. He'd go directly do his hotel room and work on his novel. "You want to be a writer? Every *putz* wants to be a writer." He headed down the flowered path that led to the main gate and walked past the tall guardsmen in their blue tunics and bearskin shakos. Before going back to his room, he'd pay a little visit to the Andersen statue. He'd spend a moment or two with Andersen. How did the old woman know of Bruno Schulz? Schulz, the tormented Polish Kafka. And how did she know Cythia Ozick? He loved Ozick. Her crazy Puttermesser character. Puttermesser, an exhausted single woman lawyer in New York working for some godforsaken city bureau makes a Golem out of her houseplant dirt to do her housework. The Golem arises from the dirt of the plant and takes over Puttermesser's life and Puttermesser runs for mayor. Ozick also wrote the great story "Envy; Or, Yiddish in America". Ozick, the mistress of *Yiddishkeit*, sometimes so impenetrable and magical that he can't understand what she's writing about. But her novel, "The Messiah of Stockholm", that was clear, a classic, easy, smooth Ozick read. The story of the lost son of Bruno Schulz working as a theater critic in Stockholm, living alone in a garret. Suddenly, the man's unknown sister appears in Stockholm clutching the manuscript of Schulz's lost novel, "The Messiah". Like Andersen's "Little Match Girl," standing barefoot in the snow. Supposedly "The Messiah" was Schulz's story of Sabbatai Zevi, the false 17th century messiah who started a messianic revolution among the Polish Hassidim. Singer wrote his first novel, "Satan in Goray", about Sabbatai Zevi. He was musing on all this in the Danish moonlight as he slowly approached the huge statue of Andersen in the square across the street, just outside the walls of Tivoli.

Should he give Andersen another little *shry* and tell him that his lost love, Jenny Lind, was back in town?

Should he tell the old Danish faery tale meister about Ozick's story of Bruno Schulz in Stockholm? Andersen, when he was dying, was befriended by a Jewish family in Denmark, the Melchior family. He was such a difficult and cranky old man living off the hospitality of his friends, most of his friends abandoned him. When Andersen was dying he made his last paper cut for the mother of the Melchior family. What was her name, the woman who nursed Andersen when he was dying? Dorothea Melchior. Dorothea and Moritz Melchior. Andersen made a beautiful paper cut for Dorothea. His final paper cut a gift to her. Marcus Melchior, maybe a grandson or other relative, was a rabbi in Copenhagen in 1943 when the Germans began their action against the Jews. He remembered a photograph of Marcus Melchior, the rabbi of Copenhagen, a tall slim professorial looking man riding a bicycle, wearing a wing collar and a foulard, a Prince Edward Hamburg and a black suit and vest.

As he stood before the statue of Andersen, he imagined Dorothea Melchior bending over the dying Danish writer, her black ringlets just touching his face, her breath, her dark eyes, infusing the old magician with another day of life. He had cut his last ballerinas for her. His last paper swans and then he cut a pair of leering skulls. He looked up at the statue of Andersen and reached out to him and touched Andersen's hand and turned and left the square and walked back to the hotel.

8

AN OLD MAN WAS BEHIND the front desk. Half asleep. He let him in the door. He didn't ask the old man if there were any messages. He took the elevator up to his room, untied his shoes and kicked them off. He hung his jacket up, sat in a chair and began to write, working on his cemetery again.

KAENE MAESCHE SWARTZSCHILD

My grandfather, Maesche Swartzschild. Maesche with the Masonic ring and the beautiful voice. He could have been a cantor. With a voice like that he could have been a *chazzan*. Instead he became a salesman. A wild, young, handsome salesman with a full head of black hair and his own carpet store at the corner of Wabash and Lake in Chicago when he was only 28. The New York Rug & Carpet Company. Maesche Swartzschild. They buried him with his Mason's ring on his ring finger, buried him beside his wife Brodie and his sister Sarah. Sarah with the round, pasty, moon face, who married a stooped, shy little man, Meier, a tailor.

What should I write about my grandfather Maesche Swartzschild? He'd lost all his money by the time the Depression hit in the early 1930s. The store, the buildings, everything. He lost it all buying Florida swampland and then started over selling life insurance policies.

One day after he'd been remarried for two years, Maesche came to see me. I was in my carrel at the university, typing a paper. I could smell the cigar smoke that preceded him. How had he gotten in the building? He had $600 stuffed in an envelope that he handed me. "Here kid, keep this for me. It's my getaway money." "Getaway?" I asked him. "From her," his new wife, the widow he married after my grandmother Brodie was killed by a train in an accident hurrying home with the chicken dinner. Crossing an unmarked crossing in the old gray Dodge. I remember the tiny red glass jewel on the light knob on the dashboard that glowed when you pulled the lights on. I also remember an album with a photograph of Maesche and Brodie in a wicker chair in Palm Beach being pushed by a black chauffeur. Maesche, who had come from the steppes of Poland, who made a fortune and blew it all gambling it away on Florida swampland and losing Chicago apartment buildings in all night poker games. My sweet grandmother, Brodie Swartzschild, crushed beyond recognition by that train. And after Brodie died, Maesche married a slack-jawed, dog-faced widow from Skokie with dyed blonde hair, Madeline. She had a face like a prize fighter, but owned a neat little Skokie bungalow where she cooked for him, she did his laundry, and baked for him. No one could equal the bakery of my grandmother Brodie. I remember the folded white powdery pockets of apricot and raspberry or the date bars waiting and still warm under wax paper on the kitchen table when I came home from school. Brodie died in that car wreck, and Maesche found himself a peroxide blonde widow with a big mouth and a nutty family. They were all supposedly rich from some sort of diet drink. A chocolate milky drink that was a substitute for a meal. "Choco-Slim."

Another afternoon soon after his marriage to Madeline and my first divorce, Maesche came up to my apartment and gave me an insurance policy with a brown savings passbook as a gift. He said he'd paid the first year's premium by forfeiting his first year's commission. After that I was to pay. If he sold enough of these he'd have a pension. He told me each year when I paid the premium I'd be adding to the cash value like a savings account. I paid the premium for three years and then I stopped. The last time I saw my grandfather, he came back to my office at the university and argued with me about my dropping the policy. His face turned red from shouting at me when I refused to renew the policy. He then asked for the $600 back which I gave to him. Six months later he was dead in a Miami hospital. Maesche, who'd get so excited he'd put his fist through his straw hat at Cub's games. He loved the Cubs and players like Ki Ki Cuyler, Tinkers to Evers to Chance. Frank Demaree. I remember my mother told me she often sat with Maesche as a little girl holding a spun sugar cone he'd bought just to keep her quiet. Maesche shouting at Billy Jurges, that anti-Semite. Hank Greenberg challenged Jurges to fight and Jurges, the coward, backed away. Kaene Maesche Swartzschild. Kaene Brodie Swartzschild. *Tak fir alt.* I was there when they lowered Maesche into his grave. The vault cover with the gold Star of David, falling into place. A miserable Chicago day of snow and ice. The rabbi handed each of us a rose to drop down into the grave. The rabbi recited the ancient Hebrew prayer, "El Moley Rachamim", and I watched a tiny old woman, huddled in her mink coat, crippled with osteoporosis, standing at graveside in her spiked heels. She fluttered some rose petals down into Maesche's grave. Who was she? A friend? An old girlfriend? Some cousin unknown to me?

When was the last time I saw Maesche alive? Was it when he came for the $600? No, after that, he separated from the second wife for a few months and took a room in a run down hotel on Wilson Avenue. I met him there in his room, reading the Tribune stock market in his undershirt, tins of tuna and sardines out on the window sill. He had no refrigerator. He seemed happy. Maesche, who had the chauffeur wipe down the steering wheel of the car with alcohol in Palm Beach each time after the chauffeur drove it, now was alone again. From the steppes of Poland to Palm Beach to a flop house on Wilson Avenue. Can I remember the sound of his voice? No. Only one word. "Dassn't. You dassn't do that." An archaic word, "Dassn't". But I can hear Maesche instructing me and I see him pointing and instead of saying, "don't do that", "you dassn't do that." "You dassn't pick those dandelions." He was a city boy. He'd never lived in a house. Always apartments. He thought the dandelions on my front lawn were little yellow flowers. I do remember the sound of his singing voice, though. All the relatives at the Seder table, sipping wine and encouraging him, "Sing, Maesche, sing." He had a deep, mournful, cantorial voice. He'd hold up his wine glass and sing. He could have sung his own "El Moley Rachamim". I could just hear his voice. "Oh G-d, full of compassion, thou who dwellest on high. El Moley Rachamim. Shochem Bahromim." He would have done a better job than the bored young rabbi handing out roses under the sleet-filled canopy waiting for his $400 check.

Kaene Mickey Bernstein

I've left out a few more memories of my uncle Mickey Bernstein, pig eyed – shrewd Mickey Bernstein, with the mouth twisted to the right side, bullnecked, a gray fedora square on his head, the brim rolled down evenly all around.

Married to my Aunt Rose, my father's sister. Heavy voiced, almost brutish, eye and mouth twisted by the stroke, stumbling as he walked away from another Seder table down Morse Avenue in the rain to a tavern. I was maybe nineteen. The family sent me after him to the tavern four blocks away to find him and bring him back. I found the tavern. He was on a barstool watching a fight on TV. "Hit 'em in the kishkes," he was yelling up at the set and knocking down shots of bourbon. He stumbled out of the bar cursing at me. I pulled him by the arm. "You know, kid, when I die I'm gonna leave you somethin' in my will. You know what I'm gonna leave you kid?" "No Mickey." "You wanna know?" "No." "I'm gonna tell you anyway. I'm gonna leave you a concession." "A concession?" "Yeah, I'm gonna leave you the hot towel concession in a whorehouse. That's what I'm gonna leave you."

And so we made our way back through the rain, up the stairs and back to the Seder. Mickey and me. "El Moley Rachamim." Mickey Bernstein. *Tak fir alt.*

Enough of the novel. It isn't any good. Just ridiculous flashes of family memories. I should get out of the room. Call Elyse Friedberg. What's her room number? I should ask her down to the bar for a drink. Another flash of Cynthia Ozick, her story, "Envy; Or, Yiddish in America". The two old Yiddish poets, one was Edelshtein. Who was the other, Baumsweig? They were both jealous of Yankel Ostrover (Isaac Singer). They went to a lecture by Ostrover. He was a *Chazer*. His stories were translated into English. He had left the world of *Yiddishkeit* and now was worshipped by the *Goyim*. An international star. Edelshtein and Baumsweig were little nobodies. Little *pippuks* compared to Yankel Ostrover. Edelshtein was probably based on the modernist Yiddish poet, Jacob Glatstein – Yankev Glatshsteyn. Singer couldn't stand the

Yiddish modernist poets of New York. He thought they were fakes. They thought he was a *goy*, a *Chazer* in the spotlight.

What was her room number?

9

HE CALLED ELYSE FRIEDBERG. She sounded happy to hear from him and told him she'd meet him in the lobby bar in ten minutes. He went downstairs and got a table away from the television set. They were still showing soccer, interviewing Danish and Dutch players from the afternoon's match. The bartender was an African-American who said there weren't many Americans in Copenhagen this year. He'd been in Copenhagen for two years and was from L.A. and liked it here and thought maybe he'd stay. He was living with a Danish woman and trying to paint.

He ordered another Carlsberg, but instead of Aquavit, he ordered a shot of bourbon, "Old Forester".

"A boilermaker," the bartender said to him smiling. "I don't serve many of these."

"Occasionally I like them."

"A real working man's drink."

He sipped some of the bourbon and went back and sat down. He thought about Elyse Friedberg. She was a refined, elegant woman, close to his age. He was tired of playing games with nymphets. He'd gotten himself involved in some kind of farcical, literary maze like a Nabokov character, and he wanted out. This woman could help lead him out. He had come to Denmark to do some serious work. The swan boat excursion and the séance were filled with grotesqueries. Leda, Mooney

Levine, Madame Josefina, the bucolic harem dancer, all still whirling around in his head. They did nothing to advance his novel. He supposedly was a serious scholar. Maybe though, the construction of the little cemetery wasn't so foolish after all. He loved the cheerful little doves the Danes put on their head-stones. He had another colorful postcard that he found lying on one of the gravel paths of Tivoli. A postcard of a little smil-ing Danish boy dressed as a gate attendant at Tivoli in an over-sized black uniform. He wore a long double-breasted coat with brass buttons and a black peaked cap with a red Tivoli hat band. Red birds were whirling around his head. Three red and orange tiny birds. Each with a sprig of a flower in their beaks. The postcard had a legend, "Det gamle trykkeri smogen Tivoli". Probably "The Little Bird Man of Tivoli". Better the three red birds whirling than the sad white chicken of *Shlogen Kapores*.

Elyse Friedberg suddenly appeared at his table and reached out and touched his hand. He could sense her perfume as she sat down.

"Hello John," she said to him.

He was drawing on a cocktail napkin.

"What would you like to drink, Elyse?"

"I'll have some white wine. Ask him if they have a pinot grigio." She looked up at the bartender. "Do you have any pinot grigio?" She had a soft, gentle manner making a request. An ab-solute contrast from her friend Martha.

"We have a pinot grigio from Venice."

"I'll have a glass of that."

The bartender brought her a glass and a dish of peanuts and another of tiny black Italian olives.

"What are you drawing John? It looks like a circle full of dots."

"Actually it's an atom. It's a drawing of a single uranium atom and its nucleus. A U235 atom."

"Is that your field? Do you teach physics?"

He put the pen down and smiled at her. "No, I'm not in science. I teach English. I'm an English professor."

"At Northwestern?"

"How did you know?"

"You're a professor and you live in Evanston, you probably teach at Northwestern." She lifted her glass to him. "I actually went to Northwestern years ago. I have an English degree too, but I never did anything with it. I got married instead."

He raised his shot glass to her. He took a sip of the bourbon and washed it down with the Carlsberg.

"*Skål*," she raised her wine glass. "Did you enjoy the séance?"

"I did. It was weird, but interesting."

"What happened?"

"Well, Madame Josefina had us all put our hands on a table and then she contacted some spirits. You know the Danish writer Isak Dinesen? She contacted her in the spirit world."

"I love Isak Dinesen. Did the Madame use a Ouija board?"

"No, she had a young woman assistant dressed in veils who would dance and twirl around to Arab music and then suddenly the voice of Isak Dinesen came into the room like a scratchy old record."

"Maybe it was a scratchy old record."

"It could have been an old phonograph hidden behind the curtain."

"What did she say?"

"She said she was looking for her lover Denys Finch-Hatton."

"I remember him in the film 'Out of Africa', Robert Redford.

He flew away from her in that old biplane and tipped his wings goodbye to her. Later he crashed into a mountain."

"Right and she buried him high on a hill where the lions he loved would come to visit him. Tomorrow night Josefina promises to bring Finch-Hatton back for Isak Dinesen if she'll bring back Hans Christian Andersen to the séance from the spirit world."

"Oh, I love him too. Hans Christian Andersen, 'The Little Match Girl', 'The Princess and the Pea', 'The Little Mermaid'. We went out to the harbor and saw The Little Mermaid, "Den lille Haufrue.""

"I haven't seen her yet. Come tomorrow night and leave your friend Martha at home. You can witness all these reunions."

"I'd love to," she said, shaking her hair away from her face, "but we're leaving early in the morning. Martha has an appointment in Stockholm with an orthopedic surgeon. She's certain that she has a torn rotor cuff and she was referred to this doctor by her doctor in Chicago. I can't stop her. She's like a bull in a china shop when she gets going. But she's one of my oldest friends. I've known her forever – grade school, high school, camp together as children."

"You've barely seen Copenhagen."

"I know. We've been here only two days and have just been shopping."

"Do you know what happened here with the Jews during the war?"

"I really don't know. Something awful I suppose."

"The Danes saved almost their entire Jewish population. There were seven thousand Jews in Denmark. They smuggled them out in fishing boats across to Sweden. Almost all of them were saved. Only five hundred were taken by the Germans. The Danes are a wonderful people. Denmark was the only country in Europe that refused to turn over its Jews to the Germans."

"I really don't know much about the history of the Holocaust. I know about Auschwitz and the concentration camps in Poland. I haven't heard the story about the Danes."

"One of the Jews rescued was Niels Bohr, who was part Jewish, the physicist who won the Nobel Prize. He was rescued and taken to the U.S. and worked on the atomic bomb at Los Alamos. He worked on the controlled chain reaction of fission."

"So you were thinking about him when you were drawing the circle with the tiny dots."

"I was."

"Was he saved by the Danes?"

"Yes, he was taken out of Denmark across to Sweden. Then he went to the Swedish king and got him to grant asylum to all the Jews who would come to Sweden."

"I feel foolish not knowing these things. I wish I had more time here. I don't think much about the Holocaust. I think more about Israel and the Palestinians."

"Before I leave Denmark I want to go up the coast and visit the harbors where the Jews boarded the fishing boats. Some of the boats have been preserved."

"If I were here and didn't have Martha in tow, I'd like to go with you." She drank more of her wine and her eyes flashed at him. Then she took his pen and a small notebook from her purse and wrote the letter of his first name "J" on a sheet of paper. "I do acrostics. I make poems out of the letters of your name. One line from each letter. I learned how to do it by watching these old men in a plaza in a town in Mexico. People would come to them for poems, for marriages, birthdays, burials or just for advice. This sweet old man had an old typewriter. The keys were bound with rubber bands. He taught me how to do it."

"J," she said, "I'll do your name Do you want 'John" or the diminutive 'Johnny?'"

91

"Do the diminutive but I call myself 'Jonny'"

"OK" J-O-N-N-Y."

"J – Just because we have only one night"

"Porque solo tenemos una noche"

"O – Only this one night"

"Solo esta noche"

"N – Never perhaps to meet again"

"Tal vez no volveremos a vernos"

"N – Never can the words be said"

"Las palabras nunca son suficientes"

"Y – I can't think of anything for 'Y'. Okay."

"No me viene a la mente nada con 'Y'.

"Yet I'm happy that we met, Jonny Levin."

"De todos modos me dá gusto que nos hayamos conocido, Jonny Levin."

She tore the sheet from her notebook and handed it to him. Her glasses were down on her nose. He read it and smiled up at her.

"Where did you learn to speak Spanish like that?"

"At Northwestern. I had three years. I love Spanish culture. In fact, Martha and I just visited Madrid."

"Madrid."

"I just love it there. We went to the bullfights, the Plaza del Toros. I think if I could be born again I'd come back as a Spaniard. I love the bullfighters. The matadors' faces. The high dark planes of their faces. I thought I'd be repelled by the killing of the bull, but I wasn't. Vaqueros, the picadors, the thrusting of the banderillos, the thrust of the matador's sword, I wasn't repelled, I was fascinated."

"I've never seen a bullfight. I don't think I want to see one."

"It's full of pageantry. I even bought these stockings

there at the corrida." She was wearing a long black skirt and she lifted it and displayed her pink stockings.

"You could be the first Jewish woman matador."

"Why not? Do you know that I was once Miss National Zeta Beta Tau? Why not a matadora?"

"Miss National ZBT? That means you were voted the most beautiful Jewish college girl in the country."

"I was never that attractive. My father was president of the fraternity's board of directors. The election was rigged."

She smiled up at him.

"Jonny. Believe me, that was another life ago. I wonder if the bartender knows how to mix a pitcher of sangria? If I order one would you have some with me?"

"Sangria, why not?"

She went over to the bar and began an animated conversation with the bartender. He couldn't hear her, but he watched her gesticulating and giving directions.

She came back and sat down.

"He'll make us a pitcher. He's got the ingredients, he's just a little rusty. He's from L.A. He said sangria's very popular in L.A."

"There must be a lot of matadoras in L.A. Do you know about Sydney Franklin? Have you ever heard of him?"

"Sydney Franklin? No, I've never heard of him."

"He was a Jewish boy from Brooklyn. His real name was Sydney Frumkin. He was the first American to be given the title of Matador in Spain."

"Really? How marvelous."

"Maybe you'll be the second."

"I don't think I could actually kill a bull. There's just a teeny little spot on the bull's shoulder where you thrust the sword. I don't think I could do it or if I tried I'd miss and the bull would kill me. Anyway, I'm too much of a coward. I've read about the great Spanish matadors like Dominguin and Manolete. I just love their faces, their sad eyes. The way they tie their hair back. The golden suits they wear. The Suit of Lights. The way they arch their backs when they thrust their swords."

The bartender brought the pitcher of sangria and set it down on the table. "It's been a long time," he said to her, "but I think I got it right." He poured them each a glass and put a slice of orange in both glasses.

"It's delicious, just right. There's a trick to drinking it Jonny. First you taste it and swish it around your mouth and hold it in your cheeks. Some people like to drink it when they make love and then spit it at each other and pretend it's blood."

"Spit blood at each other?"

"Right. If a matador is wounded by a bull, he'll suck his wound and spit his own blood back at the bull and dare him to come at him again. When the bull does, the matador has his sword hidden and thrusts for the kill. He lures the bull by spitting blood at him."

"I could ask you if you've ever done this?"

"You mean spit blood on a lover? No, but I have a friend who tied her husband to their headboard with his ties. They drank a pitcher of sangria and she pretended to spit her blood on him."

"Then she killed him?"

"No, silly. She didn't kill him. She tied him up and they made love."

"Elyse, what do you do in Chicago? Do you work?"

"Work. Oh god no. I haven't had a job in years. I taught school for awhile. And then I quit and married a very wealthy man. About ten years ago he left me for a younger woman, a trophy wife. I'm happy to be single. I travel, I take classes. I have a good life. I have a good time."

She reached into her purse and brought out what looked like a pair of black plastic scarabs. "Do you know what these are?"

"What are they, castanets?"

"Yes, castanets. I bought them in Madrid when I bought the stockings."

"You know Madame Josefina's assistant at the séance had a pair of golden castanets. She clicked them while she danced."

"Did she really?"

"Can you do anything with them? Play the castanets?"

"I've been practicing. I can do the beat of the Spanish dance Tchaikovsky wrote for 'Swan Lake'. Do you know the Spanish dance?"

"I know 'Swan Lake'. I saw it once in London in Albert Hall, the English National Ballet." He caught himself using the swan allegy again. Leda, the Swan Boat, the inn in Holland, "The White Swan," and now "Swan Lake".

"Drink your sangria Jonny. I can play these. I'll show you. I have to sit up very straight, very, very straight. Then you pull your skirt up to your knees, arch your back like a matador and close your eyes. Just cup your hand." She began to click the castanets and stamp her feet as if Tchaikovsky's Spanish dance was buzzing through her head and just then her cell phone began to vibrate on her belt.

"Oh my god, it's Martha." She playfully pinched his nose with the castanets and then reached for her cell phone which had begun chiming.

"What now?" she said into the phone.

"No, you're not having a heart attack."

"How do I know? Martha, it's just a muscle pull. Tell the doctor in Stockholm about it tomorrow and go back to sleep."

"No, I won't call an ambulance. You call the ambulance

yourself Martha. Martha – answer me. Are you really in pain down your left arm? All right, all right, call the ambulance."

She hung up and now she was angry. "Oh shit, John. She's calling an ambulance. I have to go. She just drives me crazy. I should have never traveled with her. I always feel sorry for her and give in to her. I have to help her. If she's really having a heart attack, I'd never forgive myself."

"John, I'll give you my card and when you're back in Chicago please call me. I'd really like to see you again. You seem like such a nice man. I wish I'd gone to the séance with you. Also, I would have liked to have seen those fishing boats you told me about. There'll be no Martha in Chicago. I promise." She leaned over him and kissed his cheek. She pressed her cheek against his face, and in a moment she was gone.

He looked at her card.

Elyse Friedberg
143 Harbor Drive
Chicago, IL 60601

773-861-1421   Apt. 56-H

She'd forgotten her castanets. He could run after her and give them to her. Instead he'd just keep them and maybe return them to her in Chicago. He stuffed them into his jacket pocket.

10

HE WENt BACK UP to the room. His face in the elevator mirror seemed mottled and scabrous. Maybe it was just the dim light of the elevator or the blacking of the mirror had begun to fleck away. He took the castanets from his pocket and posed in front of the elevator mirror. "Just arch your back," she'd said. He tried a few clicks as the elevator ascended. He could combine them with a few Zulu tongue clicks, or better yet, some of Borge's tongue clicks. What would Victor Borge do with a pair of castanets? He'd build a whole act around them. The elevator door opened and he found his key and opened the door to his room.

The light was on. Leda was lying on his bed reading one of his books.

"Leda, how did you get in here?"

"The old man at the desk let me in. I told him I was your daughter."

"Well, get out. Get out now. I don't want you in here. I want you to leave."

"Where can I go? My landlady won't let me back in. I gave her the 300 kroner you gave me and she still won't let me in. She wants 4,000 kroner. She's got all my things locked up. Even my bird is locked away in my room. She's got a brute of a half-wit son, Mikos. He's locked up all my things, my clothes, my bird, my dishes, all my paints and brushes and my massage oils. Jonny, please help me. Jonny, give me another 3,700 kroner. I'll

97

pay you back in a week, I promise. You can't be poor if you can afford to stay in this hotel and you have all these books and clothes."

"Give me that book, Leda." He reached for it and she held it away from him.

"No, it's very interesting to me. You have this page marked at this photo. I know this photo. My friend Iphigenia's father has the same photo in their home. This man here," she pointed to a figure of a young man holding a rifle in the photograph, "that's Iphigenia's father. He was a partisan in the last war." She pointed to the photograph of a young man wearing an armband guarding a group of women, moving them down the street. There were several men in the photo with rifles, all wearing the same armband. "Where did you get this book, Jonny? I swear this photo is the same photo. That man is Iphigenia's father. He has the photo framed on their mantelpiece."

He took the book out of her hands.

"What do you mean that man's your friend's father?"

"It's him, Iphigenia's father. Simon Braucivius. A very bad man. A drinker. A wife beater. He beat all of his children until one night Iphigenia attacked him with a heated rod from their fireplace. He left her alone after that. She took off as soon as she graduated from the gymnasium. Now she's in Riga with a husband and two children. Simon Braucivius lives across the street in Kaunas from my parents. Iphigenia's mother is gone, dead for years. Her sisters live in Poland. He lives there with some young whore who helps him drink up his pension and has a lover who is a police officer."

"Leda, I think you spin these fables like a little spider. You just exude this thread of fantasy and wrap it around everybody and everything at your will."

"Exude? What is that? Spin fables like a spider? I don't know what you mean."

"Iphigenia is a name right out of Euripides. You're a story teller."

"Thank you. To me, that is a compliment. We studied Euripides and now, I remember, we teased Iphigenia about her name. Her mother gave it to her. It's a beautiful name."

"This man, you say his name is Simon? He's still alive?"

"I don't know if he's still alive. I haven't been home for three years. He was alive when I left. He was just an awful man. I never spoke to him. Neither did my parents. When I was a child I was in Iphigenia's house all the time. We avoided him. He stayed mostly in his basement in his workshop with his shortwave radio. But the photograph of him is as a young soldier, a partisan. He was very proud of it. I'm amazed that you have it in your book. Where did you get such a book? A collection of photographs like that?"

"These men weren't Lithuanian partisans Leda. They were killers. Jew killers. The women they're herding down the street are Jewish women. They're leading them to their death. Probably to trucks that will take them to the Ninth Fort (IX Fort) or the Seventh Fort (VII Fort), the old czarist forts in Kaunas where the Jews were executed by the Germans and their Lithuanian helpers. Or maybe to Ponar, the forest outside of Vilnius. Probably not to Ponar. It would be too far. Do you know Ponar? Have you been there? Do you know the Seventh or Ninth Forts?"

She looked at the photograph again. "I know of the Ninth Fort. Everyone in Kaunas knows of that fort. I've heard of Ponar but I've never visited the forest there. Oh no, we went there once in a bus from the school. I remember now. You say these are Jewish women? That these Lithuanian men killed them? That is untrue."

"It is very true."

"There is a plaque at the forest in Ponar, I remember it,

but it is in memory of those killed by the Communists, not in memory of Jews."

"So you don't think Lithuanians killed Jews? Who do you think these women in the photograph are?"

She held the photograph up to the lamp beside the bed.

"They are Lithuanian women. These men are saving them from the Germans. They're leading them to safety."

"That's what the man Simon told you? Your friend's father told you that?"

"Yes, he had a medal for that. Also in a case on the mantel. He and his fellow partisans. See the man in the beret standing beside the women directing them? I also knew him. He is dead, though. I know him to be dead. He was a friend of my father and taught English at the gymnasium. He taught me English. My father drank with him at the same tavern. He was a good man, a very kind man. He would never kill people. He would never hurt anyone."

"Do you see the armbands all the men are wearing?"

"Yes."

"They're all wearing the same armband, a tri-color. Perhaps the colors of Lithuania's flag. What are those colors?"

"Yellow, red and green, but I cannot tell. It's all gray in the photo."

He put the book back down on his dresser and pointed to the door.

"All right Leda, get out. Enough of the history lesson. These men weren't Jew killers, they were brave Lithuanian partisans. I want to go to bed and I want you out of here now."

"I won't go. I will only go if you give me 3,700 kroner. Give it to me as a loan or as a fee. I will even take you to Lithuania to Kaunas as your guide. I will show you where Simon Braucivius lives. I will introduce you to him if he's still alive."

"Leave before I pick you up and throw you out."

"Jonny, you would not do that to me," she laughed at him. "You're too much of a gentleman. Please give me the money. I will pay you. I promise. I swear I will repay you."

He thought of grabbing her ankles and pulling her off the bed and he put his hands around her ankles, but she kicked free and held onto the headboard and laughed again.

"You're not strong enough, Jonny. No man is strong enough to push me around if I don't want to go. Except perhaps Mikos, the landlady's son. He's a moron and a real brute. You're not a brute. Also, you're not a moron."

He looked at her and decided she was right. If she resisted him there would be no way he could pull her off the bed and force her out of the room. But it would be worth 3,700 kroner just to get her out of his room.

"I'll give you the money," he said. "Stand up."

"I won't stand until you hand me the money. Put it in my hands."

He went to his suitcase and unzipped the compartment where he'd put the Danish money he'd changed. He'd changed $750 and he still had almost $600 in Danish currency. He counted out 3,700 kroner and dropped the bills down on her hands. She watched him drop the notes and when he finished she pulled his head down and kissed him full on the lips.

"Go now," he said to her. "Go."

"Don't be so harsh, Jonny Levine. See, I remember your name. I will go. I will contact you tomorrow, though. I will make further arrangements with you. You will be paid."

She got up and walked to the door and she turned back to him and put her arms around him.

"You know, you still have that delicious scent, Jonny Levine. The odor of America. The allure of wealth, capitalism and great power. I am leaving. You will see. I will repay you. We will become great friends. You will learn to trust me." She stood in the corridor for a moment and then she was gone down the stairs.

Yes, he was a moron, a fool to have given her the money. He turned all the lights out except the reading lamp over his bed and kicked his shoes off. He took the book and opened it to the marked photograph, the one of Jewish women being herded down the street by armed Lithuanian men. There was another photo of Jewish men being beaten to death by Lithuanian thugs wielding iron bars in a square in Kaunas. A crowd of Lithuanians and German soldiers was watching and laughing. There was another of Jewish men at the old fort in Kaunas. The Jewish men were standing in line on the abutments of the fort, pressed up against each other, their undershirts pulled up over their heads as hoods, moving forward toward a killing squad. He'd become obsessed with these photographs. He looked at the photograph of the women. There were about six Lithuanian men with rifles standing beside them. The man with the beret was the leader. He was the one Leda said had been her English teacher. He was holding a stick, like a whip, and was bending forward shouting orders at the women. The women were of all ages, young girls, mothers, grandmothers, children, simply dressed. The man she called Simon was to the right. He looked about twenty and he wore riding boots and an open-throated white shirt. It was summertime. The sun was on his face. A perfect, bland Slavic face. High cheekbones, Mongol eyes, and showing no expression.

All the men with rifles seemed easily identifiable. He'd written several letters, one to his senator, another to his congressman, another to the American ambassador to NATO. A kind of Bellowian collection of letters. Right out of Herzog.

Each of them answered him politely. Had these men ever been arrested and prosecuted, he'd asked in each letter. Had they ever been identified and made to stand trial for their crimes? Why admit Lithuania to NATO and to the European Union with these men, these killers of Jewish women, still walking around free? Why? The answers were all polite. Bureaucratic politesse. Inquiries would be made. He would be advised. Identities would have to be confirmed. These were events of over sixty years ago. Many of the accused were probably dead. Proofs would have to be established. His letter to the Simon Wiesenthal Foundation enclosing copies of each photograph was unanswered. He'd kept a copy of his letter in the book.

No answer. No response from Simon Wiesenthal. Only more solicitations for contributions from the Simon Wiesenthal Center. He'd sent them $100 with the photographs.

He'd tried to reach the president of Lithuania, Valdas Adamkus, a Chicagoan who'd returned to Lithuania after many years in America and was elected president. One of the professors in the history department, his friend, Marty Feinberg, went to a dinner in honor of Adamkus, but Marty, self-promoting Marty, did nothing. "It really wasn't possible, John," "It really wasn't propitious." Marty remained silent. Marty was a bull-shitter.

There was another photograph that he'd marked, but Leda had missed it. It was in a collection of pre-Holocaust photographs of Jewish children in Poland and Lithuania by the photographer Roman Vishniac. A photograph of a group of young Jewish boys and girls ages about twelve or thirteen, a group of young students standing in a doorway waiting for the school doors to open. They were all well-dressed. The girls wore dresses and knee stockings with sandals. Some had fashionable haircuts, mostly shorn on the neck and worn in a bob in the back. The boys wore shirts and ties. All the students were frozen in a moment, eating, talking, gossiping, waiting for the school to open. He would summon forth the photograph and the faces of the young students would be with him as he searched for sleep. Had they survived the holocaust? Was the photograph taken in Poland or Lithuania? What had happened to all these young Jewish students? Had they been killed? He would never know. But he had also brought the Vishniac book of photographs with him to Denmark. The two photographs were secretly etched into his memory, almost like crystalline etchings. The group of young students and the bland, remorseless, dead expression of the young Lithuanian man with the rifle.

It would be difficult, but tonight he would expunge the face of the man and call forth only the faces of the young students and try for sleep with only their faces haunting him. He would expunge Leda, Elyse Friedberg, the whirling dancer of the séance, Madame Josefina, Mooney Levine, the few paragraphs of his novel, the man in the beret, and the man with the rifle. He'd find the faces of the students standing on the stairs and they would remain with him and hopefully he would weave them into a dream where they would still be alive.

A
Commuter's
Notes

L · B · K

1

TODAY ON THE WAY TO THE STATION from the office as I passed under the El tracks at Wells and Washington, I saw a man dressed in a clown suit behind the wheel of a black car that was waiting for the light As I crossed Wells, I looked up and staring at me from the driver's seat of a black car was a fully made up clown. He wore a ruff collar. His face was creamed white, with black and red lips, and red circles daubed on his cheeks. I think he wore glasses. He was dressed in a red and white striped clown's suit and his ruff was white and crinkled like the collar of an ancient English Queen, or a Renaissance Duchess. As I passed the car and glanced at him again, his nose lit up and flashed at me. He must have had a hidden button that he could touch to make his nose flash. A red bulb on the tip of his nose flashed white, on and off, and he stared directly at me, unsmiling. He looked like John Gacy, "The Killer Clown", reincarnated. The four men behind me, lean, older men, dressed in almost identical black suits, saw him and laughed.

109

Then, on the way to the station, they continued discussing a dissent of Justice Antonin Scalia. One of them said, "It's nice to read something that makes common sense." None of them mentioned the clown.

* * *

My name is Alfred Witkofsky. I'm 55 years old and a lawyer with offices on the 22nd floor of a building on Michigan Avenue in Chicago. I'm a solo practitioner and I have a small corporate, probate, and real estate practice. I'm married to Bettina who I call Betts. She's a sculptor and ceramicist and designs lamps for a company in Northfield. We live on the North Shore in Highland Park. We have one son in high school, a 16-year old named Tom, Thomas Witkofsky.

* * *

If I ride two trains a day, five days a week (10), for fifty weeks a year (500). and have been for 30 years, apparently I've ridden the train 15,000 times. I hope these notes have the feeling of a person on a train. A sense of disjointed anonymity and voyeurism. Short and long jolts. The constant sounds of the announcements, many of them automated, station stops, safety warnings, warnings of doors that don't open, doors that are open, apologies for being late, breakdowns before us, breakdowns after us, holiday schedules, on and on and on. Also, the conductors, some bullying and curt, calling for tickets, rapping on the railing with their metal ticket punches. Others civil and friendly. I hope to get it down, the sudden lurching, passengers sleeping like corpses wearing head sets, mouths gaping open. Mindless talk of golf across the aisles.. Young people with back

110

packs, eager to get off, up and standing in the aisle. Some stay back and sift through the garbage bins for the morning paper. Some of the older passengers also sift the garbage or walk the cars looking for papers. I'm usually one of the last to get off.

* *

At breakfast, I ask Charmaine, the French waitress, if the word in French for grapefruit is *palempousse?*... "No," she shakes her head, *pamplemousse, pamplemousse.*" She said it twice. She's a lovely, auburn-haired Parisienne in her forties. She works downtown in a restaurant on Monroe Street. I don't know what she's doing there. This morning, as I was leaving, she said to me, "*Le travaille est le sanité.*" Work is sanity

* * *

It's the next morning and I don't think I'll stop to see Charmaine. I have to be in court for a Probate hearing. There's a man across from me this morning on the upper deck on the 8:05 dictating into a tiny, black microphone looped around his neck .. "Hello, Sandra. ... I'm on the 8:05." He's also writing on a yellow legal pad on his knee. A young girl in jeans and sandals, about fifteen, sitting across from him, stares at him for a moment and then returns to her paperback and snaps her gum. Another man begins using a cell phone. When he dials, the sounds are like dart points whirring through the quiet of the car.

* * *

A woman gets on in Wilmette and immediately takes out her cell phone from her purse and dials. She doesn't seem to care if anyone overhears her. She keeps talking all the way into the city. As soon as she hangs up from one call she makes another. A woman in her fifties, a blonde with hoop earrings, a wide mouth and a huge shiny, black leather handbag. The man behind me, encouraged by her, pulls out his cell phone and calls his office. "Is Peter there? He isn't there yet? Well this is Steve and I'm late. I'll be there about 9:20. If there's an expert named McCarthy sitting in Reception, tell him I'll be a few minutes late. Offer him some coffee   Okay?" Okay seems to be the command buzzword used in different tones of modulation. "Okay,", he says more abruptly and hangs up. I think he's a lawyer with an expert witness waiting for him. I didn't mind the call. Not one call, but a few minutes later, he was back on his phone again. I wanted to turn around and snatch it out of his hands.

* * *

If I ride two trains a day, five days a week (10), for fifty weeks a year (500), and practice law for fifty years before I retire, I will have ridden the train 25,000 times. If I spend an hour on each ride, I will have expended 25,000 hours commuting, or over 1,000 days. That would be three years of my life sitting on the train. I say that I'm writing these notes as a sort of diary of what it's like to be on a train for a portion of each day of your life. I don't think I'm really doing that. I'm just writing about myself, and the sudden lurches, the disjointed paragraphs are not from the train.

* * *

It's Friday night and the beginning of the weekend. A man in an immaculate blue suit, sits across the aisle from a younger man. The older man speaks in a loud voice. "Read your memo today." The younger man is very attentive. Perhaps, a senior partner in a law firm speaking to a young associate. The partner wears a white handkerchief in his breast pocket and an American flag pin in his lapel. He's neatly barbered and has a tan and looks very healthy except his left eye has a bad tic. The younger man is pale and has tousled hair and needs a haircut. He gets off in Evanston with a polite nod of his head to the older man. The young lawyer probably lives in a small apartment with a wife and a kid in diapers. The partner gets off in Kenilworth and waves to his wife who's wearing sun glasses and is parked in an emerald green Mercedes.

* *

At Hubbard Woods a man sets his briefcase down to stoop at the edge of the platform to pluck a white flower. It looks like a white wheel made of lace. Queen Anne's Lace.

* * *

It's Monday morning. I have a will and a trust to complete today. My client isn't married. He's been divorced for many years. Very few men really get down to human matters in a will. A woman usually takes great care to leave things to specific people. She'll give away her jewelry, piece by piece (my antique ring to my niece Paula, my gold wedding band to my granddaughter Kimberly). She lovingly details each gift, (my living room rug to

113

my son Anton, my dining room rug to my son Casimir, my coffee maker to my friend Eugenia my cookbooks and copper pots to my sister Carla) Women's faces shine with the joy of giving when they detail these gifts. They really seem to be at peace with themselves and the concept of death. Lately, some of my women clients have been giving away parts of their bodies, eyes to the University of Chicago, kidneys to the Kidney Foundation, bodies to Northwestern University Medical School to be used as cadavers. Not so the men, they seldom make personal gifts or direct that organs be given to medical research. The men don't want to talk about death. They talk about "passing away." or "if I should go." or "if something happens to me." The men are interested in money and taxes.. They want to know about estate tax impact and generation skipping. They don't want to talk about death, so I don't mention it.

* *

On the 5:45 Tuesday evening, I see an African American boy out the window near the Clybourn station with a butterfly net, a white net on a long pole. He's crouched over in a weed thatch in a vacant lot alongside a factory.

* * *

The French waitress at the restaurant on Monroe Street, used the personal form in speaking to me today for the first time. She handed me my bill and said "Pour toi." She probably wasn't even conscious of saying it. I've been there so often recently, I must seem like one of her friends. I think it's time we began using the familiar form. I'd use it when speaking to her, but I don't know how to decline the verbs properly. She has beautiful eyes and

114

as she bends toward me to take my coffee order she looks at me. "Vos yeux sont belles." "Your eyes are beautiful," I should say to her. I don't know if that's right. It might mean, "your eye is beautiful". I try to think of what to say to her before I see her, because my French is so poor, I have to have the phrase firmly in mind. So usually, on the way down on the train, I'll try to imprint a French phrase so I'll have the sentence ready at breakfast. "Vos yeux sont belles" was the phrase for this morning. I didn't use it though.

* * *

I had lunch with one of my friends today, a lawyer who has the same kind of practice that I do, except that he's also a litigator. I don't try many cases. I have a few. I'm really a desk lawyer, an office lawyer.

My luncheon partner and I have been friends for a long time. I asked him if he spends as much time as I do worrying about money. I think some of these notes are just a conceit or a mask. I really spend much of my time worrying about money. I paid my office rent today. I have $1,600 in my checking account after paying the rent. I billed about $6,500 this month. That's a good month for me. I usually bill about $5,000. You ought to be able to live in the suburbs on $6,500 in monthly fees and my wife's salary from the lamp company of thirty thousand. I don't find it easy. I'm always fighting to pay my mortgage and my credit cards. I don't have a regular secretary. I have an arrangement with a woman I've known for many years and she comes in for emergencies. I usually do my own word processing and I've become quite adept at it. Some days though, I feel that I'm not really a lawyer and all I do is stenography. I've been a lawyer now for almost 30 years and I've never had a salary check. I've always had to worry about making money. So why am I trying to hide it?

115

I read the other day, that some partners in large Chicago firms had a share of profits last year in excess of a million dollars. What would I do with that kind of money? I guess I'd set aside a trust for Betts and another for our son, Tom. He's an oboe player in the high school orchestra and wants to go to the Juilliard School in New York. I'd love to send him there. He has real talent. When he plays his oboe solos, the audience becomes hushed and his notes are so plaintive and lovely that my eyes often brim with tears. I also read this morning that one of the large firms in Chicago is dissolving and that the partners may not get their pensions. What would I do if I worked all my life and my firm closed and I lost my pension? I think I'm better off where I am, practicing alone, although I'm sure I'm viewed as an anachronism. I probably am, but at least I'm my own anachronism.

* *

On the 7:48 this morning. I had to climb a little hill. up a path through the weeds in order to catch the train. There was another man ahead of me, heading up the embankment, for a moment we were each lost in the tall cool weeds like children in the overgrowth at the edge of a playground.

* * *

At a real estate closing this morning, the buyer had no lawyer, he said he'd had too many bad experiences with lawyers. He was from New York, a heavy man with red, flushed, mottled cheeks and narrow eyes. He'd been transferred to the Midwest as a Regional Sales Manager of a kitchen ware company. He and his wife were buying a condominium on the North side that an estate owned. His broker represented him at the closing and when

116

I handed over the Bill of Sale from the Executor, the real estate broker said to his client, "This transfers the personality of the condo." I laughed, "Personalty," I said to them, "not personality. You can't transfer the personality." I don't think they understood.

* * *

Later in the afternoon, I walked over to La Salle street to a law firm for a settlement conference on a reformation suit. It's one of my few pieces of litigation The suit claims both parties had mistakenly computed interest on a mortgage. The lawyer for the defendant offered me $50,000 as a settlement. When I got back to the office and called my client in Texas he told me, "That's a low ball offer. Sec if you can get some more."

A client, a woman, called me today. She was incensed that I had charged her for phone calls in her divorce case. I've gotten out of divorce. She was one of my last divorce clients and I represented her in a post decree hearing. Her husband had his alimony reduced. He'd lost his job and his new job paid $20,000 less. He got a reduction and the woman was outraged. I just let her rave on and on. I could hear ice clinking in her glass. She started to sob, then she'd take a drink and start crying again. Finally I hung up on her. I don't have to take abuse from clients. Some clients are really neurotic and make impossible demands on lawyers. Also some are greedy and dishonest and there's nothing you can do to satisfy them. You should learn to weed them out and never get involved with them. I'm working on a difficult contract and I don't want to be interrupted because the woman is angry and lonely. 1 charged her fairly. I'm not a therapist.

* * *

Sunday, a white butterfly hovered over me in the back yard. It was the first butterfly I'd seen in our back yard this year. I thought of the white butterfly on the inside cover page of the book we have of drawings by the children in the concentration camp in Terezin in Czechoslovakia, "I Never Saw Another Butterfly". Betts and I were in Prague a few years ago but we didn't go to Terezin. I didn't want to see it. We have the book in our den at home and after I saw the butterfly, I went upstairs and looked at the inside cover. Actually, the butterfly is white, but the child tinged its wings with orange and put blue polka dots on each wing.

* * *

At breakfast on Monday morning when Charmaine poured me a refill of coffee, I thanked her and said, *"Vous etês très chere."* She laughed. "I'm very expensive? *Très gentille.* you mean."

She set my English muffin down in front of me.

"You once said to me, *'Le travaille est la sanité,'*" I said to her.

"Yes."

"Do you really believe that?"

"Yes."

"*'Arbeit Macht Frei'.* Do you know what that means?"

"No, I don't understand German."

"It means the same as *'Le travaille est le sanité.'*"

"But that is true," she said patting her hair in place.

* * *

After breakfast, on the way to LaSalle Street I passed by a new bank. There was a man in front of the bank dressed in a gorilla costume, standing in the rain with some young women who were passing balloons out to promote the opening. The poor man must have been soaked inside that gorilla suit. I thought the bank would have more class than to open up in the rain and force a man to stand there in a gorilla suit. I could meet Charmaine some night for a drink if I dressed in a gorilla suit, but I don't think so. I'll never meet her. Betts would never forgive me. Even if I dressed as a minotaur, half man and half beast, I don't think my costume would protect me.

Picasso was good at portraying men as minotaurs. I could diseuss Picasso with Charmaine, my voice resonating from inside the simian chamber, "Do you know, Charmaine, that the painting by Picasso, 'Les Demoiselles d'Avignon,' really portrays women in a bordello in Madrid by that name? Picasso was probably a patron there. The women are so sad and exploited. He recognized that. That's why their faces are so angular and their huge, sad eyes are bulging out of their sockets." On some of Bett's abstract busts of me, I look like one of these women.

* * *

The next morning. It stopped raining and the sun came out. In order to celebrate summer, instead of going right to work, I detoured a block and walked over to the Bank One Plaza to visit the Chagall Mosaic. I hadn't been there all winter because the stairs were icy and the colors are hidden in the gray weather.

119

But today all the colors of Chagall were vivid in the sunlight. I looked for the golden ballerina and at first I couldn't find her. I didn't have quite the right angle. Then, suddenly, I moved a few paces and there she was, flashing at me in her golden bodice. I also walked around the monument to find the bluebird, and I found her, full-breasted blue and yellow, hidden in the branches of a tree. And beside her, a falling angel coming down from heaven, diving toward the silhouette of the City and Lake Michigan. Further on, around the corner, I found the beautiful red cardinal, above two lovers embracing. I visited the musicians, the fiddlers, clarinet players, and the dancers. You have to remind yourself of joy and how to be ecstatic and alive. I was alone, all alone with Chagall's artistry, standing in the canyon of glass skyscrapers. No one else was there. I was the only one in Chicago there. Only one person passed, a young woman on her way to work, dressed in a raincoat, talking on her cell phone, her heels clicking, a black bag over her shoulder. She didn't even glance at the Chagall. Also, the bank has put another clock there, 9:04.

2

I HAVE JUST REVIEWED these notes. I think I'm making a mistake by writing about my life in short paragraphs. It interrupts the flow for the reader. Anyway, I think I can tell myself and the reader more if I occasionally write a page or two about my observations, instead of just short paragraphs. Not so much, my observations, but myself within those observations. I don't know if that's clear but I'll try. For instance, this morning on the 8:05, as I was re-reading my first chapter, a friend coming up to the upper deck of the train interrupted me. I was glad to see him. He's a senior partner in a large firm. He told me that in order to fit into that kind of law practice, one has to "learn how to do the numbers." I suspect there's a lot more to it than that but my friend has been through a lot of medical procedures recently. He had an angioplasty last Friday and here he was on the train going down to his office. He seemed very pale and after we reached Chicago he touched me on the shoulder and when we said goodbye on the station platform, I suddenly had the feeling that I would never see him again. I'm too sensitive. I know that. I get these premonitions and they're very frightening.

When I left him and walked down the platform to the station and the bus, as his pale face faded, I began to think further about my first chapter and how it stood up to what I was actually seeing as I passed through the station. I think it's much too fragile. I don't spend my time looking at flowers. There're too many references to flowers. The city is much too brutal to permit that kind of thinking. When you step out of the station, you step into real life. There are beggars waiting for you jingling the coins in their paper cups. The noise and the fury of the city hits you immediately and my musings on beauty and Queens Anne's Lace seem foolish. On the bus with my cup of Starbucks decaf cappuccino with skim milk and a shot of vanilla, I seem very insignificant. The great face of the city is on the bus. It's mostly Hispanic and black and Indian and Asian. A family from Mexico was seated across from me. It was nice to see a family together, grandfather, teen-age grandson and granddaughter and the grandfather's son and wife. In the suburbs you only see that grouping in the restaurants, usually with the grandfather as the host. The children were very respectful to their grandfather and they all got off the bus together at Randolph and Michigan and the grandson held the door for me. I said thank you and he answered "You're welcome." Then as I crossed Michigan Avenue on the "Walk" sign, I passed in front of a row of cars and taxis, all stopped and waiting for the light. Any one of the drivers could have tapped his accelerator and run me over. If that happened, it would be the end of this story and maybe you would say. . . "Good, we don't have to read what Alfred Witkofsky is thinking about anymore." But one thing that Alfred knows is that there are almost no blacks or Hispanics in the suburbs, and the face of the city is largely black and Hispanic. Chicago is one the most highly segregated cities in the country. Also the law firms of Chicago, the major firms, employ almost no blacks and Hispanics as lawyers. That's a dirty little secret of the legal profession and although I'm quite good about writing about the fragility of flowers, I only mention an African American once in the opening chapter and that's the boy I saw trying to capture a butterfly in his butterfly net.

Today, I actually confronted one of the cell phone callers I find so offensive. I was almost alone in the car on the way into the city; perhaps there were three or four other people. A man in his late 40's started using his cell phone. He was very brash and loud and I looked over at him several tines and he seemed to lower his voice and then he quickly ended the conversation and I returned to my paper. I like to read the New York Times in the morning and I leave the Chicago Tribune at home for Betts. Then suddenly he pulled out his phone again and made another call. His voice grew louder and louder and he was almost shouting. I stood up and leaned across the upper deck and asked him to lower his voice. "Sir, would you please lower your voice?" He paid no attention to me. I asked him several times. Finally he looked up at me and mumbled something. I began to lecture him. "This is not your office. This is a train. We aren't interested in your personal affairs, we don't want to be intruded upon." He said something else to me but he was very annoyed. I finally said "that if he had lowered his voice, I wouldn't have minded, but he showed no civility or courtesy." I went back to my seat. Of course, the other passengers, all men, hid behind their papers. They wanted nothing of this confrontation. He said to me as I sat down, "This is a public car." I then leaned across and exploded, "I've been riding these trains for thirty years and I don't have to listen to this kind of bull shit." We both then lapsed into silence but I could feel my heart thudding. My adrenaline was really pumping. He got off in Evanston without looking at me. I was glad he got off. I didn't want a confrontation when I got off in Chicago. I guess I finally have had it. One cell phone call too many. I come across sort of as a wimp in the opening chapter, but I'm not that way at all. I'm tough and can be very argumentative and confrontational. I guess that's why I've survived as a lawyer.

Awful pain from sciatica. This p.m. had to get down on the floor to pull my legs to my chest to get rid of it. I couldn't find my big pillow, the one that I've had for years, covered in a silk texture. I have a Danish modern office chair and it's very hard, not comfortable for a client to sit on, so I cover it with the soft pillow. I couldn't find the pillow and immediately decided that the cleaning lady had stolen it. I'm becoming so paranoid. She's a very nice woman, always beautifully dressed when she comes to work, a silk scarf around her throat. Why would she steal my pillow? I did find it under another chair and I did my leg to chest pulls prone on the floor on my back and the sciatica diminished. I'm waiting for a messenger to deliver a $13,000 fee to me. The first installment of my attorneys fee on a million three hundred thousand estate. I've been trying for three weeks to collect from the bank named as Trustee. The total fee will be $39,000 and this will be the first installment of three payments. I billed them on October 1 and then they asked me to amend my statement and give them another summary of my time, which I did and now, supposedly, they'll messenger the $13,000 fee to me this afternoon, We shall see. I've been around too long to trust them fully. Something will probably come up to delay the payment.

Last night I met an old friend on the 4:35 on the way back from the city. He's a lawyer. I think he's a partner in a small firm. He was a tough kid who grew up on the West Side. In the last few years he's taken to wearing baseball caps to the office. I think that many men as they grow older begin wearing hats that reveal their secret yearnings. Some wear cowboy hats, or sea captains' hats, Greek fishermen caps, berets, Sherlock Holmes hats, Borsalinos, floppy canvas camper hats, college caps. Lately, I also have been wearing a baseball cap. I played baseball in high school. Although recently I switched to a University of Michigan Alumnus hat that reads "Michigan Billiards." I used to hang around the billiard room to shoot pool. People occasionally stare at me. One woman on Michigan Avenue looked at me and called out, "Go Blue." I didn't know what she was talking about. That expression didn't exist when I was an undergraduate at Michigan.

My friend is very garrulous. He also sang with a swing band to put himself through law school he told me, and though I've never heard him sing, I'm sure he has a beautiful voice. His practice is something like mine. He doesn't have a secretary. I think he's made money in real estate and probably owns buildings and doesn't have to practice law. Anyway, he began to talk about how much he loves his wife. How his heart thuds every time she meets him at the train, even though they've been married 40 years. I asked him how they met. He said a law school classmate fixed them up. When she came to the door on that first date, he knew that she was the girl he was going to marry. They went out for dinner and then went for a walk in the park. I forgot to add that when he picked her up her father was in the living room playing the mandolin. I asked him if he sang for her father.

He said no, but later when he was walking his wife through the park, he sang for her. I asked, "do you remember the song?" He said, "Yes, 'The Anniversary Waltz', I sang it to her and we danced. It was just an excuse to hold her in my arms." I hummed a bar for him and he smiled and said, "You got it."

Later, when I told another lawyer friend the story about how my friend's heart thuds when he sees his wife at the station waiting for him, he said to me, "Maybe he should see a good cardiologist."

* * *

One of the conductors loves to make announcements. I think he thinks he has the voice of a radio or TV announcer, he sounds like one and is constantly droning away about emergency exits, keeping your feet off the seats and watching your step because platforms may be slippery or wet. Today it was, "don't forget your parcels" day. Only he's added a new warning. "Please, ladies and gentlemen, with the world situation as it is today, please don't leave your parcels on the train. Also report any untended baggage to your conductor." Also, in the station, a man in a black T-shirt walking with a sniffer dog. His T-shirt was labeled "K-9." On the bus today, the driver stopped for a woman who didn't have a ticket but was looking for Wabash Ave., which was only three blocks away. He told her to "Get on the bus, I'll take you there." She said, "There's seven of us." He said, "Okay, get on" and then she waved to six young black women waiting at the stop and they all got on the bus. "We have to catch a flight, ladies," she said to them. They were all urban poor. They were silent and wide-eyed, dressed in sweatshirts and jeans. I had on my University of Michigan Billiards cap and felt a little foolish. I thought of asking one of them where they were going, but I didn't.

None of them carried any luggage. They seemed very apprehensive and perhaps this was their first plane trip. The city has an entirely different face on the bus. This morning I was the only white person; all the riders were either black, Asian, or Hispanic. I said "good morning" to a Hispanic man about my age sitting across from me as I sat down. He smiled graciously at me and answered, "good morning."

* *

I don't think I've mentioned that I play the harmonica. I have a Red Hero (Made in China) harmonica in my wall cabinet in the office that I haven't played in years. Every time recently that I open the cabinet, I see the harmonica there and I've been tempted to blow a few riffs. Today when I opened the cabinet, the harmonica actually fell out onto the metal filing cabinet. It was as if it was beckoning to me to play, so I did play, and I chose "My Old Kentucky Home," which I played quite well if I say so myself.

* * *

Betts and I are going to London for ten days later this month. I did get that good fee from the bank and I booked tickets on British Air. We're staying at a small hotel near Hyde Park, right on the edge of Hyde Park along Bayswater Road. I have always wanted to go to the Round Pond in Hyde Park and sail a toy sailboat with the British children and fathers who sail their boats there. I walked over to Marshall Fields this afternoon to see if I could buy a small wooden sailboat. I wanted to paint Betts' name on the stern. "Betts-Chicago." I couldn't believe that Marshall Field's toy department, which used to cover almost half a floor, has shrunk down to a tiny little section in the toddlers'

126

clothes department. There was nothing there resembling a toy sail boat. Maybe I'll find one at Harrods.

Today as I prepared to get off the train, I watched a small man, about 45, in a yarmulke, a black *kippah*, sifting through the garbage bin to make up a complete Chicago Tribune. I was up on the 2nd deck in my favorite seat, which is the 1st double on the right hand side, and I watched him below assembling his morning paper from the discards in the bin. He was very quick and adroit although he seemed so frail to me and I thought how he would have appeared in the Berlin of the 40's with his black *kippah*. He wouldn't have lasted very long. It made me think of Charmaine and my conversation with her about *Arbeit Macht Frei*. I know that the Germans used to march daily in Paris down the Champs Elysees and I should have asked whether anyone ever told her about those parades? I think often about the Holocaust, particularly when I pass the cemetery where my parents are buried. The family came here from Lithuania in about 1870, my great grandparents. They came from Mariampole. My parents were completely assimilated and as children were given formal religious training but never were very observant. We always celebrated the holidays with dinners and family gatherings, but my parents seldom went to a synagogue. I remember going with my father when I was a child to an old synagogue in Rogers Park where he would say Kaddish for his mother. Other than that, my parents seldom attended services except for funerals and I had no religious training. But those members of our family who stayed in Lithuania were never heard from again after the Holocaust and I assumed they all died. I remember my aunt had been in touch with a woman cousin who was a dentist in Mariampole and they corresponded frequently but after the war there were no more letters. I saw her photo once, she was a plain faced, kindly looking woman who wore a pince nez and a high collared black dress.

I have always had a desire to return to Mariampole to try to learn what happened to the members of our family. I have done some research and I've found the diary of an SS officer, Standarten-fuhrer Karl Jäger, who compiled the so called "Jäger Report" list-ing city by city the number of Jews killed by his units and Lithuanian "partisans" under his command. It is a daily list and on September 1, 1941 he notes that in Mariampole 1,763 Jews, 1,812 Jewesses and 1,404 Jewish children were killed. I've seri-ously considered a trip to Lithuania to try to learn more about this. I wonder if some of the so-called Lithuanian "partisans" who took part in the killings may still be alive and at large. I sup-pose I'm being foolish to think I could track them down. I have some old photos of these men and maybe I could start with those and bring them to the attention of our government, our Ambas-sador to Lithuania, and ask that they be shown to local police or prosecutors or advertised in the newspapers. In the past, I have written the Simon Wiesenthal Foundation about the men in these photos but had never received a reply until recently. I think I'll also send the photos to the Wiesenthal Foundation. I have at-tached the Jäger Report as an exhibit to this story so that the reader can refer to it.

I've even bought a small paperback book I found in a trav-el store with names of Lithuanian people who'd like to correspond with people from other countries. They invite people to come to their homes and stay with them. If I went to Lithuania, I might stay with some of them. Most of these people weren't even alive during the Holocaust. As an example, a woman teacher in Vilnius, born in 1952 writes: ". . .I live with my family in a seven-storey house not far from the city centre. I love fishing, camping, and traveling. I have pen friends in many different countries. You are welcome!" She speaks English, Russian and Italian. ". . .ex-changes assistance, bed 11 p.m. and breakfast 7:30 a.m." (She sounds like a nice lady, but I don't think I'd like the requirement of bed by 11 p.m. and breakfast at 7:30.)

Here's another, a man or woman, I can't tell because the Lithuanian names are difficult. A computer programmer, ". . .I am unemployed and will be pleased to entertain guests. I can help them understand our life in Vilnius and help with business here. I collect stamps, metal badges, and souvenirs of wood and amber. Speak English and Russian. Bed and breakfast for 1-2-3-4 persons." (I'd probably be a good guest with my multiple personalities.)

And another, age 54, a university teacher, ". . .I am an elderly lady of a sunny disposition, interested in England and Scotland. I could take you to the seaside in summer. Speak English, Russian. Interested in music, theatre and books."

I don't think I would ask any of them to take me out to Ponar, the forest outside of Vilnius where the Jews were executed. I wouldn't want anyone with me. I don't know if I could really stay with a Lithuanian family. Maybe I would erupt in anger and make a scene, or do something that they don't really deserve as my hosts. No, I'd go to Ponar alone. There are also several forts in Kaunas, old Czarist forts that were killing places of Jews. I wonder if they even have plaques there. There are three volumes in the Highland Park Library about the Jews of Vilnius and there are photographs that show how the Jews were buried in the pits of Ponar, stacked in tiers. In these photographs it looks like some kind of lime has been poured over their bodies. There was a plaque put up there after the war by Vilnius Jews in the memory of the Jews murdered at Ponar, but it was torn down during the Russian occupation. Supposedly, now there's a museum at Ponar. I have a photograph of Jewish women being herded by Lithuanian guards in Kaunas. The guards are dressed in civilian clothes and wear armbands. Some of the faces of these men are very recognizable. High-planed

Slavic faces, straight blonde hair slicked back. All the men wear the same armband. It looks like a kind of tricolor. Also there's another photo of killing pits in a forest with several naked Jewish men and a naked little Jewish boy of about seven wearing a cap about to be shot by men in civilian clothes apparently wearing the same armbands.

I would ask my hosts if these men in the photographs have ever been identified? Have they ever been brought to trial? Who were they, these Jew-killers? Where are they today? Are they still walking the streets of Vilnius and Kaunas or even Mariampole? . . . Perhaps I should stay at a hotel. I don't want to ask my hosts questions like that.

*　*　*

I have the listing from the People to People book for Mariampole (Marijampolu).

The first person listed is a nurse. She's about 38 and she speaks English and Polish. She offers assistance, bed, and breakfast. She likes history, knitting, and animals.

The next is a man, a civil engineer. He's about fifty and also offers assistance and bed and breakfast. He enjoys "sports, guitar, theatre." Speaks English, Polish, and Russian. He's fifty. He was born in 1955. I'm fifty-five, so we're almost the same age. I can speak a little Polish. Maybe I should stay with him.

Or perhaps with a student who's the third person listed. I can't tell from the first name if it's a man or a woman. Again the same languages spoken. This person though is interested in theatre, literature, and UFOs but I'm not sure about the UFOs.

Finally, there's a woman, 36 years old, speaks Polish and Danish. How would we communicate? She's a teacher though, a teacher of Lithuanian language and she's probably quite intelligent.

130

I could write all four of them and tell them that I'm coming to Lithuania and see if any of them reply.

What would I say to them. . . ?

That I want to come to Lithuania to find out how my family died in the Holocaust?

Did they know that on September 1, 1941 that 5,000 Jewish men, women, and children were killed in Mariampole?

What would they say to me? None of them was alive on September 1, 1941, sixty-four years ago.

I would ask them if they knew anything about the killings of the Jews of Mariampole? Have they ever been told anything? Where were they killed? In a forest? Were they taken to the forest at Ponar in Vilnius? Were they taken to the old Fort in Kaunas? Or were they killed in Mariampole?

I would show them the photos I have of Lithuanian men leading Jewish men and women down the streets or herding them into killing pits. Are these Lithuanian men still alive? Do you recognize any of them? Where can I find them? Who would know of them?

They would probably say—this happened years before I was born. How would I know of them?—But then I would ask them about their parents. They were alive during the war. They would now be in their eighties or late seventies. Some of the parents must still be living. I know American men who fought in World War II and are still alive. Let me speak to your parents. I would say, I will learn Lithuanian to speak to them.

I have already learned a few words in Lithuanian that I would say to them.

Good morning —*Labas rytas.*

My name is Alfred Witkofsky—*Mano vardas yra Alfred Witkofsky.*

What's your name? —*Koks Jūsu vardas?*

The
Jäger Report

The Jäger Report

Commander of the security police and
the SD Einsatzkommando 3
Secret Reich Business 1 December 1941
Kauen [Kaunas]
5 copies
4th copy

Complete list of executions carried out in the EK 3 area up to 1 December 1941

Security police duties in Lithuania taken over by Einsatz-kommando 3 on 2 July 1941.

(The Wilna [Vilnius] area was taken over by EK 3 on 9 Aug. 1941, the Schaulen area on 2 Oct. 1941. Up until these dates EK 9 operated in Wilna and EK 2 in Schaulen.)

On my instructions and orders the following executions were conducted by Lithuanian partisans:

4.7.41	Kauen-Fort VII	416 Jews, 47 Jewesses	463
6.7.41	Kauen-Fort VII	Jews	2,514

Following the formation of a raiding squad under the command of SS-Obersturmfuhrer Hamman and 8-10 reliable men from the Einsatzkommando. the following actions were conducted in cooperation with Lithuanian partisans:

7.7.41	Mariampole	Jews	32
8.7.41	Mariampole	14 Jews, 5 Comm. officials	19
8.7.41	Girkalinei	Comm. oficcials	6
9.7.41	Wendziogala	32 Jews, 2 Jewesses, 1 Lithuanian (f.), 2 Lithuanian Comm., 1 Russian Comm.	38
9.7.41	Kauen-Fort VII	21 Jews, 3 Jewesses	24
14.7.41	Mariampole	21 Jews, 1 Russ, 9 Lith. Comm.	31

135

17.7.41	Babtei	8 Comm. officals (inc. 6 Jews)	8
18.7.41	Mariampole	39 Jews, 14 Jewesses	53
19.7.41	Kauen-Fort VII	17 Jews, 2 Jewesses, 4 Lith.Comm, 2 Comm. Lithuanians (f.), 1 German Comm.	26
21.7.41	Panevezys	59 Jews, 11 Jewesses, 1 Lithuanian (f.), 1 Pole, 22 Lith. Comm., 9 Russ. Comm.	103
22.7.41	Panevezys	1 Jew	1
23.7.41	Kedainiai	83 Jews, 12 Jewesses, 14 Russ. Comm., 15 Lith. Comm., 1 Russ. O-Politruk	125
25.7.41	Mariampole	90 Jews, 13 Jewesses	103
28.7.41	Panevezys	234 Jews, 15 Jewesses, 19 Russ. Comm., 20 Lith. Comm.	288
		Total carried forward	3,384

Sheet 2

		Total carried over	3,384
29.7.41	Rasainiai	254 Jews, 3 Lith. Comm.	257
30.7.41	Agriogala	27 Jews, 11 Lith. Comm.	38
31.7.41	Utena	235 Jews, 16 Jewesses, 4 Lith. Comm., 1 robber/murderer	256
31.7.41	Wendziogala	13 Jews, 2 murderers	15
1.8.41	Ukmerge	254 Jews, 42 Jewesses, 1 Pol. Comm., 2 Lith. NKVD agents, 1 mayor of Jonava who gave order to set fire to Jonava	300
2.8.41	Kauen-Fort IV	170 Jews, 1 US Jewess, 33 Jewesses, 4 Lith. Comm.	209

4.8.41	Panevezys	362 Jews, 41 Jewesses, 5 Russ. Comm.,14 Lith. Comm.	422
5.8.41	Rasainiai	213 Jews, 66 Jewesses	279
7.8.41	Uteba	483 Jews, 87 Jewesses, 1 Lithuanian (robber of corpses of German soldiers)	571
8.8.41	Ukmerge	620 Jews, 82 Jewesses	702
9.8.41	Kauen-Fort IV	484 Jews, 50 Jewesses	534
11.8.41	Panevezys	450 Jews, 48 Jewesses, 1 Lith. 1 Russ.	500
13.8.41	Alytus	617 Jews, 100 Jewesses, 1 criminal	719
14.8.41	Jonava	497 Jews, 55 Jewesses	552
15-16.8.41	Rokiskis	3,200 Jews, Jewesses, and J. Children, 5 Lith. Comm, 1 Pole, 1 partisan	3207
9-16.8.41	Rassainiai	294 Jewesses, 4 Jewish children	298
27.6-14.8.41	Rokiskis	493 Jews, 432 Russians, 56 Lithuanians (all active communists)	981
18.8.41	Kauen-Fort IV	689 Jews, 402 Jewesses, 1 Pole (f.), 711 Jewish intellectuals from Ghetto in reprisal for sabotage action	1,812
19.8.41	Ukmerge	298 Jews, 255 Jewesses, 1 Politruk, 88 Jewish children, 1 Russ. Comm.	645
22.8.41	Dunaburg	3 Russ. Comm., 5 Latvian incl. 1 murderer, 1 Russ. Guardsman, 3 Poles, 3 gypsies (m.), 1 gypsy (f.), 1 gypsy child, 1 Jew, 1 Jewess, 1 Armenian (m.), 2 Politruks (prison inspection in Dunanburg	21
		Total carried forward	16,152

Sheet 3

Total carried forward 16,152

Date	Place	Description	Total
22.8.41	Aglona	Mentally sick: 269 men, 227 women, 48 children	544
23.8.41	Panevezys	1,312 Jews, 4,602 Jewesses, 1,609 Jewish children	7,523
18-22.8.41	Kreis Rasainiai	466 Jews, 440 Jewesses, 1,020 Jewish children	1,926
25.8.41	Obeliai	112 Jews, 627 Jewesses, 421 Jewish children	1,160
25-26.8.41	Seduva	230 Jews, 275 Jewesses, 159 Jewish children	664
26.8.41	Zarasai	767 Jews, 1,113 Jewesses, 1 Lith. Comm., 687 Jewish children, 1 Russ. Comm. (f.)	2,569
28.8.41	Pasvalys	402 Jews, 738 Jewesses, 209 Jewish children	1,349
26.8.41	Kaisiadorys	All Jews, Jewesses, and Jewish children	1,911
27.8.41	Prienai	All Jews, Jewesses, and Jewish Children	1,078
27.8.41	Dagda and Kraslawa	212 Jews, 4 Russ. POW's	216
27.8.41	Joniskia	47 Jews, 165 Jewesses, 143 Jewish children	355
28.8.41	Wilkia	76 Jews, 192 Jewesses, 134 Jewish children	402
28.8.41	Kedainiai	710 Jews, 767 Jewesses, 599 Jewish children	2,076
29.8.41	Rumsiskis and Ziezmariai	20 Jews, 567 Jewesses, 197 Jewish children	784
29.8.41	Utena and Moletai	582 Jews, 1,731 Jewesses, 1,469 Jewish children	3,782
13-31.8.41	Alytus and environs	233 Jews	233
1.9.41	Mariampole	1,763 Jews, 1,812 Jewesses, 1,404 Jewish	

		children, 109 mentally sick, 1 German subject (f.), married to a Jew, 1 Russian (f.)	5,090
		Total carried over	47,814

Sheet 4

		Total carried over	47,814
28.8-2.9.41	Darsuniskis	10 Jews, 69 Jewesses, 20 Jewish children	99
	Carliava	73 Jews, 113 Jewesses, 61 Jewish children	247
	Jonava	112 Jews, 1,200 Jewesses, 244 Jewish children	1,556
	Petrasiunai	30 Jews, 72 Jewesses, 23 Jewish children	125
	Jesuas	26 Jews, 72 Jewesses, 46 Jewish children	144
	Ariogala	207 Jews, 260 Jewesses, 195 Jewish children	662
	Jasvainai	86 Jews, 110 Jewesses, 86 Jewish children	282
	Babtei	20 Jews, 41 Jewesses, 22 Jewish children	83
	Wenziogala	42 Jews, 113 Jewesses, 97 Jewish children	252
	Krakes	448 Jews, 476 Jewesses, 97 Jewish children	1,125
4.9.41	Pravenischkis	247 Jews, 6 Jewesses	253
	Cekiske	22 Jews, 64 Jewesses, 60 Jewish children	146
	Seredsius	6 Jews, 61 Jewesses, 126 Jewish children	193
	Velinona	2 Jews, 71 Jewesses, 86 Jewish children	159
	Zapiskis	47 Jews, 118 Jewesses, 13 Jewish children	178

5.9.41	Ukmerge	1,123 Jews, 1,849 Jewesses, 1,737 Jewish children	4,709
25.8-6.9.41	Mopping up in: Rasainiai	16 Jews, 412 Jewesses, 415 Jewish children	843
	Georgenburg	all Jews, all Jewesses, all Jewish children	412
9.9.41	Alytus	287 Jews, 640 Jewesses, 352 Jewish children	1,279
9.9.41	Butrimonys	67 Jews, 370 Jewesses, 303 Jewish children	740
10.9.41	Merkine	223 Jews, 640 Jewesses, 276 Jewish children	854
10.9.41	Varena	541 Jews, 141 Jewesses, 149 Jewish children	831
11.9.41	Leipalingis	60 Jews, 70 Jewesses, 25 Jewish children	155
11.9.41	Seirijai	229 Jews, 384 Jewesses, 340 Jewish children	953
12.9.41	Simnas	68 Jews, 197 Jewesses, 149 Jewish children	414
11-12.9.41	Uzusalis	Reprisal against inhabitants who fed Russ. partisans; some in possesion of weapons	43
26.9.41	Kauen-F.IV	412 Jews, 615 Jewesses, 581 Jewish children (sick and suspected epidemic cases)	1,608
		Total carries over	66,159

Sheet 5

		Total carried over	66,159
2.10.41	Zagare	633 Jews, 1,107 Jewesses, 496 Jewish children (as these Jews were being led away a mutiny rose, which	

		was however immediately put down; 150 Jews were shot immediately; · 7 partisans wounded)	2,236
4.10.41	Kauen-F.IX	315 Jews, 712 Jewesses, 818 Jewish children (reprisal after German police officer shot in ghetto)	1,845
29.10.41	Kauen-F.IX	2,007 Jews, 2,920 Jewesses, 4,273 Jewish children (mopping up ghetto of superfluous Jews)	9,200
3.11.41	Lazdijai	485 Jews, 511 Jewesses, 539 Jewish children	1,535
15.11.41	Wilkowiski	36 Jews, 48 Jewesses, 31 Jewish children	115
25.11.41	Kauen-F.IX	1,159 Jews, 1,600 Jewesses, 175 Jewish children (resettlers from Berlin, Munich and Frankfurt am main)	2,934
29.11.41	Kauen-F.IX	693 Jews, 1,155 Jewesses, 152 Jewish children (resettlers from Vienna and Breslau)	2,000
29.11.41	Kauen-F.IX	17 Jews, 1 Jewess, for contravention of ghetto law, 1 Reichs German who converted to the Jewish faith and attended rabbinical school, then 15 terrorists from the Kalinin group	34
EK 3 detachment in Dunanberg in the period 13.7-21.8.41:		9,012 Jews, Jewesses and Jewish children, 573 active Comm.	9,585

141

EK 3 detachment in Wilna:

12.8-1.9.41	City of Wilna	425 Jews, 19 Jewesses, 8 Comm. (m.), 9 Comm. (f.)	461
2.9.41	City of Wilna	864 Jews, 2,019 Jewesses, 817 Jewish children (sonderaktion because German soldiers shot at by Jews)	3,700
		Total carried forward	99,084

sheet 6

		Total carried forward	99,804
12.9.41	City of Wilna	993 Jews, 1,670 Jewesses, 771 Jewish children	3,334
17.9.41	City of Wilna	337 Jews, 687 Jewesses, 247 Jewish children and 4 Lith. Comm.	1,271
20.9.41	Nemencing	128 Jews, 176 Jewesses, 99 Jewish children	403
22.9.41	Novo-Wilejka	468 Jews, 495 Jewesses, 196 Jewish children	1,159
24.9.41	Riesa	512 Jews, 744 Jewesses, 511 Jewish children	1,767
25.9.41	Jahiunai	215 Jews, 229 Jewesses, 131 Jewish children	575
27.9.41	Eysisky	989 Jews, 1,636 Jewesses, 821 Jewish children	3,446
30.9.41	Trakai	366 Jews, 483 Jewesses, 597 Jewish children	1,446
4.10.41	City of Wilna	432 Jews, 1,115 Jewesses, 436 Jewish children	1,983
6.10.41	Semiliski	213 Jews, 359 Jewesses, 390 Jewish children	962
9.10.41	Svenciany	1,169 Jews, 1,840 Jewesses, 717 Jewish children	3,726

16.10.41	City of Wilna	382 Jews, 507 Jewesses, 257 Jewish children	1,146
21.10.41	City of Wilna	718 Jews, 1,063 Jewesses, 586 Jewish children	2,367
25.10.41	City of Wilna	1,776 Jewesses, 812 Jewish children	2,578
27.10.41	City of Wilna	946 Jews, 184 Jewesses, 73 Jewish children	1,203
30.10.41	City of Wilna	382 Jews, 789 Jewesses, 362 Jewish children	1,553
6.11.41	City of Wilna	340 Jews, 749 Jewesses, 252 Jewish children	1,341
19.11.41	City of Wilna	76 Jews, 77 Jewesses, 18 Jewish children	171
19.11.41	City of Wilna	6 POW's, 8 Poles	14
20.11.41	City of Wilna	3 POW's	3
25.11.41	City of Wilna	9 Jews, 46 Jewesses, 8 Jewish children, 1 Pole for possesion of arms and other military equipment	64

EK 3 detachment in Minsk from
28.9-17.10.41:

Pleschnitza Bischolin	620 Jews, 1,285 Jewesses, 1,126 Jewish children and 19	
Scak Bober Uzda	Comm.	3,050
		133,346

Prior to EK 3 taking over security police duties, Jews
liquidated by pogroms and executions (including
partisans)   4,000

                                                           Total   137,346

Today I can confirm that our objective, to solve the Jewish problem
for Lithuania, has been achieved by EK 3. In Lithuania there are no
more Jews, apart from Jewish workers and their families.

143

The distance between from the assembly point to the graves was on average 4 to 5 Km.

I consider the Jewish action more or less terminated as far as Einsatzkommando 3 is concerned. Those working Jews and Jewesses still available are needed urgently and I can envisage that after the winter this work force will be required even more urgently. I am of the view that the sterilization programme of the male worker Jews should be started immediately so that reproduction is prevented. If despite sterilization a Jewess becomes pregnant she will be liquidated.

(signed)
Jäger
SS-Standartenfuhrer

1. Further information about the Jäger Report can be found on page 234 (et seq.) *The Holocaust: A History of the Jews of Europe during the Second World War,* by Martin Gilbert, Holt, Rinehart &Winston, New York, 1985.

2. Karl Jäger committed suicide before facing trial. He died in his cell at Hohenasberg Detention Center on June 22, 1959. See *Masters of Death: The SS Einsatzgruppen,* by Richard Rhodes, page 276, Vintage Books, a Division of Random House, 2003.

A
Woman
in Prague

L · B · K

HE SAW HER COMING DOWN the long path between the graves. She was a slim woman with gray hair. When he approached her he asked her if she spoke English.

"Yes, a little."

"Do you know where the grave of Franz Kafka is?"

She gestured to him to follow. She seemed to be about his own age, in her mid—50's, with once darker hair, streaked by gray. The graves had mostly German—Jewish names, Strauss, Friedlander, Schwarzchild, Weiss. The cemetery was wildly overgrown, and the lanes along the graves were long dirt paths winding under the archway of trees, almost like tunnels edged by foliage and the dark stones.

She pointed. "There, you see it? Dr. Franz Kafka." She nodded and folded her arms.

It was a simple brown granite gravestone with three names, Dr. Franz Kafka, Hermann Kafka, and Julie Kafka, in that

149

order. Below it was a newer, flat black marker with faded gold letters, also with three names, Gabriele, Valerie and Ottilie. There were pyres of small stones left on both graves as gifts from visitors, also some coins and a small bouquet of dried flowers. At the foot of the grave someone had left a plant that now had a single red blossom.

"His youngest sister's name was Julie," he said to the woman.

"No, I believe Julie was the mother."

"I'm sorry, you're right. Ottilie was his youngest sister. The three sisters died in the camps. They're not buried here."

The woman pointed to a marker on the cemetery wall opposite the Kafka grave.

"Yes, I see. Max Brod. He was his good friend."

"Yes, Brod was his friend."

She sat down on the bench along the wall.

"How long have you been in Prague?" he asked her.

"How long?" She began to count on her fingers. "*Acht*, no, in English, eight days, yes, is that right, eight? I am sorry but my English is not good."

She seemed very sad, she had a thin face etched by sadness. She was dressed in beige slacks with a gray sweater and a brown saddle leather strap purse.

"You are English?" she asked him.

"No, American. I live in New York and teach at a University there.

"Oh, yes, New York."

"And you?"

"I live in Germany. I teach the children that do not speak." She gestured with her hand to her mouth.

He sat down beside her on the bench.

"Many stones," she said to him.

150

"Yes, many. Kafka is almost an industry here." He stooped and found a small white stone and leaned over and dropped it on the rows of stones. "There are some coins there, too."

"Coins?"

"Yes, people have left coins.

"Oh, I didn't see."

He pointed to the names on the stone. "He is above his father here."

"I don't know if he would like being here with his family. I don't really know." She lit a cigarette.

He thought of a photograph of Kafka and his three sisters, the sisters in immaculate white dresses, all with dark piercing eyes and severe expressions. They didn't look like young people.

"Where do you live in Germany?"

"Live? It is in Heidelberg."

"I live in Manhattan."

"Yes. That is the city?"

"No, it is a section of New York."

"English is quite hard for me."

"I speak some French, but you speak English very well."

"No French, please. My French is awful." She grimaced and touched the ashes off her cigarette.

It was very quiet. There was only the muted sound of traffic beyond the walls, nothing else. "We apparently are alone, the only two people here," he said to her after a few moments.

"The only two? I don't understand."

"We, you and I." He pointed to both of them. "At this moment the only two who are with Kafka."

"Oh, I see. Yes. Perhaps. The only two. I think not, though." She pointed to the row of stones. "And Brod." She nodded at the marker on the wall.

There were several lines of Czech on Max Brod's memorial. He recognized the word for editor, *Redaktor*, and showed it to her.

She turned and he watched her face as she turned, a long, angular face, and dark eyes. She was still a beautiful woman. "Do you speak any Czech?" he asked her.

"No, nothing. A few words."

"Have you always lived in Germany?"

"No. I am from Hungary. I am Hungarian."

"Are you Jewish?"

"Half." She made a slicing movement with her hand and ground her cigarette out. "Half Jewish and half Christian."

"I am Jewish."

She nodded and looked away down the path. An older man in a flat cap and blue workman's clothes was coming on a bicycle. He bobbed his head to them as he passed.

"I think most of the Jews of Prague are buried here, those that didn't die in the camps," he said.

"Probably most. But also in the Old Jewish Cemetery there are many graves. This is the new one."

"I was in the old cemetery this morning. I've never seen anything like it. Graves from 1400. Rabbi Judah Lowe is buried there. The miracle rabbi who created the Golem to save the Jews of Prague. I put a stone on his grave."

She smiled for the first time and looked up at him. "I put, too. I was at the Old Jewish Cemetery and I also saw —- is that right -— saw?"

"Yes .

"The grave of Rabbi Lowe. But where was his Golem during the Holocaust? I have not seen one living Jew in Prague, only gravestones."

"I met some Prague Jews this morning, at the synagogue up the street from the Old Cemetery."

"I have been eight days here and I have not met one living Jew. Only here now, you, and you are American."

"I would like to find a bookstore that has some Kafka material," he said. "I was told there are bookstores on Wenceslaus Square. Do you know where Wenceslaus Square is?"

"Yes, I know these stores."

"Would you care to go there? Did you come on the Metro?"

"Yes, I could go with you. Why not?" She put her purse over her shoulder and stood up. They began to walk away and then suddenly she turned back and called to him. She pointed to several stones on top of Kafka's monument. "You see, one of them is not a stone at all, there it is—how do you call that in English?"

"A snail."

"I have been observing it all the time we have been speaking. Since we first sat down it has moved from here to here." She traced a line of about six inches.

"Wait just for a moment."

"No," she said. "If you watch them, they won't move at all."

"Where do you think it came from?"

"I think it came down from the trees. On threads, they come down." She fluttered her fingers.

He looked up at the trees. It would serve him right to meet a woman like this, who knew about snails that descend on silken threads from trees. He would have to come to Prague to find her at Kafka's grave.

"There are raspberries here too," she said.

"And the snails eat the raspberries?"

"No. I ate them. I picked some. They were very good. And the little ones that are crazy for the nuts, what do you call them in English, they also eat raspberries."

"Squirrels."

"Yes, in Italian, *scoiattolli.*"

153

As they walked out to the cemetery gate she pointed at several stones decorated with praying hands.

"Those are the signs of the Levites, the hands at prayer," she told him.

On the Metro, sitting silently beside her, he thought about the suicide of Primo Levi. Levi admired Kafka. He owed it to Levi to come here to Prague to Kafka's grave, and now he had met a woman, a very strange, sad woman, almost as strange and sad as himself. She hadn't told him her name and he hadn't asked.

At Wenceslaus Square she took him to a large bookstore and asked to see any books by Kafka in English. She asked in German.

"We have none," the young man in spectacles said.

"None?"

"No, we have no books by Kafka."

"In Deutsch?" she asked.

"No. None."

"No books at all by Kafka?"

He shook his head.

She shrugged, and they walked out, back into the sunlight and the crowds of people in the square.

"We will try another store," she told him.

At the second store they were taken by a young woman to the manager. "Do you have anything by Kafka in English for the gentleman?" she asked again in German.

"No, madam."

"In Deutsch? In Francais?"

"No, madam. None at all."

"In Czechish?"

"No, madam. Not for three years. There is nothing by Kafka in Prague."

"Nothing at all?"

"You will find nothing here."

They left the store and watched some children dancing to rock music in unison in lines under a loudspeaker in front of a record store. They were mostly little blonde boys and girls and they were laughing and doing the steps with their hands on their hips, their eyes bright with excitement.

"Are you surprised?" he said to her and touched her arm.

"I don't believe it. I know one more store. It is over there. I remember it as a literary store. More literary."

A man holding books he was putting up on shelves looked at her without expression. She asked him the same question.

"I am sorry, we have nothing here by Kafka."

"You have nothing at all?"

He shook his head and turned back to the shelf. "He is not available here. No." He bowed slightly with a trace of a smile.

"Ask him if they have anything by Primo Levi."

"No," he said with the same expression, "we do not have Primo Levi."

"Do you have his brother, Carlo Levi? *The Christus is Coming to Eboli?*" she said.

"No."

He asked her to join him for dinner, and they went to a tavern and had some Pilsener beer and duck. The tavern was crowded with a busload of German tourists. The men were drinking shots of slivovitz and became quite loud. After dinner he suggested to her that they leave and have dessert elsewhere.

It had become dark and they walked back to the main boulevard and had sherbet in a small cafe edged by bushes along the sidewalk. She told him a little about herself. She was born in Hungary but had fled the Germans and was saved by the Russians and then went to Italy as a refugee. She was in Venice in the winter. "It was winter," she said, drinking her coffee. "I was 12, I had no money, nothing in the purse. I was what you call an orphan —

yes, orphan. We lived in a shack. There was snow on the gondolas. I remember I wanted to taste Coca Cola. I had heard of it but had never tasted it. To me it represented freedom. So I finally had a Coca Cola, but it was awful. I hated it. It tasted like poison. Now we have eight McDonalds in Heidelberg and the place for the pizza?"

"Pizza Hut?"

"Yes, a Hut of Pizza has now also come to Heidelberg. She was staying on the outskirts of the city in a private home. "I told *Cedok* that everything they offered was too expensive. I asked them if they had a mission in the train station. They finally found for me a private house. I have a room. It is quite far from here."

She had asked him no questions about himself. Suddenly, as he paid the bill, she turned to him and asked quietly, "Are you a married man?"

"No, I'm not married. I'm recently divorced."

"I am a married woman," she said. She lit another cigarette.

"Where is your husband?"

"He is home in Heidelberg with our daughter."

"You are in Prague alone?"

"One can be quite alone in marriage."

"Yes, and also out of marriage. Kafka, better than anyone, I think, could write about the pain of being alone."

"He was very good with pain," she said. "Perhaps that is why they have banned him here now. Banned, is that right?"

"Yes."

They walked to the Charles Bridge and crossed the old bridge with its ancient statues of saints and the huge castle in the background. There were fishermen below with flat boats in the black water, and white swans on the river. Students were sitting in one of the niches of the bridge and were drinking beer and holding candles, singing quietly to a guitar.

"It would have been very hard for a Jew to hide here," he

said to her. "Almost impossible. Everyone is blonde. A Jew with dark features couldn't hide."

She stood looking down at the river. "When the Germans came to Hungary it was late in 1944. We were living in a house. I was a child. The Germans counted ten. Everyone who was ten had to go. I survived several such counts. But why the Jews went willingly, I do not know. I still do not know. Both of my parents went. I was left alone, only with my cousin. I had in my pocket like this —" she gestured "a small — how do you call it — nail file." She pretended to hold it in her hand. "I would not let them take me. After my parents went I swore that if the Germans came to me as a ten, I would do like so." She thrust her hand out. "I would kill whoever came to take me." She turned to him. "You see, I think the Jews felt they had a special bondage with God." She linked her hands. "You know the symbol of Levites? They thought this bondage was special and never could be broken. So the Jews went willingly. God would take care of them." She moved her hands apart and stared at them. "But He didn't." She sighed and shook her head. "I shouldn't talk to you about such things. You are right. It was very difficult to hide. Almost impossible." She turned to him. "It's late. I should go now. You do not have to come to the Metro. We can say goodnight here."

"No, I want to come with you."

They walked together down along the bridge through the darkness, past the students holding candles, to her Metro stop where they said good night. When he shook her hand, he was surprised at the strength of her hand. It was the hand of a worker, not a woman who taught children. They exchanged cards. After she left he looked at the card she'd given him under the streetlight. She had written her name, Nathalia. Her name, but not her address.

A
Woman
in Warsaw

L · B · K

HE WAS IN WARSAW for the International Book Fair. He'd never been in Warsaw before and he stayed at the Hotel Victoria and on his last night, after dinner downstairs, he went up to the Casino and had a brandy at the bar. A woman immediately moved over and sat beside him. She was quite beautiful, about 28, with gray eyes, very thin, with long brown hair, and dark stockings, dressed in a suit, like a young businesswoman.

"I am tired of the Germans here at the bar," she said in perfect English. "You're not German; I heard you speaking English."

"No, I'm American."

"Good. I like Americans."

He was a divorced man of 48 who owned a small academic publishing company in Baltimore. He had the face of a scholar with a high forehead, and gray hair, thinning and long at the back of his neck. He felt too tired to talk to her. He'd read in the *International Herald Tribune* of the death yesterday of

Isaac Bashevis Singer. If she was a prostitute, he didn't want to get involved with her. On his last night in Warsaw, he only wanted to drink his brandy and then perhaps find a cab and take it to Krochmalna Street, the street where Singer lived in Warsaw as a young boy. He'd promised himself that before he left he'd go to Singer's Krochmalna Street and to the Warsaw Ghetto monument. He had to be in London tomorrow afternoon.

Then he surprised himself by saying to her, "I'll buy you a drink, but I'm leaving."

"Americans are always in a hurry. Where are you going?"

"To visit friends."

"You have friends in Warsaw?"

He nodded.

"I'll have a vodka." She called to the bartender who brought over a bottle of Wyborowa. She drank down the shot and looked at the man defiantly and brushed her hair back as it fell across her face. "Are you a Jew?"

"Why do you ask?"

She spread her pale fingers next to his on the bar. "See how dark your fingers are beside mine. Most of the Americans who come here to the hotel are Jews. They come to walk on the ashes. Have you come to walk on the ashes?"

"What business is it of yours?"

"It is my business. We have a large industry in ashes." She looked at him again. "I will take you to see the Ghetto in a Mercedes."

"I'm not interested."

"Not interested in what? I do not believe you. You do not look like a man who is not interested." Her gray eyes were very beautiful. She reached to the top of her hair and pulled her dark glasses down and lit a cigarette. As she bent her head down he noticed that her hair was really auburn colored, and as she leaned

162

toward him, it brushed against his cheek. He wanted to reach out
and touch her hair, but instead he got up and put two 50,000
zloty notes on the bar.

"You will leave me here with these foolish German
tourists?"

"Perhaps I'll see you later." Then he touched the back of
his fingers to her hair and then to her cheek. It was a consciously gentle gesture, but she angrily moved her face away from him
and turned her back to him.

Outside the hotel he walked across the street to the plaza
with the Tomb of the Unknown Soldier and stood with some
people watching two young guards goose-step in cadence before
the tomb. He stared at the soldiers' high-boned Slavic faces and
their tri-crowned hats with chin straps, white gloves, and gleam-
ing black boots. There was no sound other than the hollow cadence of their marching. He watched them for another minute,
then turned away from them and found a cab.

He could speak a few words of Polish, enough to give
simple directions. "Krochmalna Street," he told the driver. The
word for street was *ulica*. "Ulica Krochmalna." It was an old cab
and the driver was a middle-aged man with thick glasses. He
drove in silence for only five or six blocks and pointed to a building on the corner. There was a sign on the side of the building,
Krochmalna Street. He got out of the cab and asked the driver to
wait for him.

The Warsaw Ghetto had been destroyed by the Germans in
1943. Every building was burned. Before World War I, Singer's father, a rabbi, brought his young family from a small town in the
provinces to Warsaw and they lived on Krochmalna Street. As he
walked along Krochmalna Street he saw only apartment buildings
with dark courtyards, a few with strands of wash hanging over the
balconies in the courtyards. A family was sitting on a front stoop

of a building. There were two blonde children, with tiny, inquisitive, fragile faces, sitting with their parents who quickly glanced up at him. He nodded to them and slowly walked back to the cab as they watched him. Before he got in he touched the bricks of the corner building.

He didn't know the word for monument. "Ghetto Monument," he said. The driver seemed to understand and touched his hat. He turned on his lights and drove to the Ghetto Monument. When they arrived, after a few blocks, the driver parked the cab under some trees at the curb, dimmed his lights and lit a cigarette.

There was a large park where he got out, and he immediately saw the silhouette of the Ghetto Monument. He approached from the rear, down a long walk. The monument was in a clearing of several city blocks, surrounded by apartment buildings. Supposedly it would be the only monument in Warsaw without flowers strewn at its base. Someone at the Book Fair had told him that all the saints and cardinals and Polish military heroes would have flowers on their monuments, but the Ghetto Monument would be barren. There had been an old woman in front of the hotel selling flowers. He could have bought her last bouquet. She held it up to him as he passed her, but he shook his head.

He walked around to the front of the statue. There were some flowers lying at its base, a sheaf of dried red flowers. He picked up one, a red flower with a black throat, and put it on the arm of the figure of the man who was prostrate, lying with his head on his arm. Then he stood back with his hands clasped in front of him and bowed his head and tried to say a prayer in Hebrew. He knew only a few words of the Kaddish, the mourner's prayer. He looked up at the faces of the statue, a young man, bare chested, his coat thrown open, holding a grenade, and a young woman behind him holding a rifle. The commander of the Ghetto forces in 1943 was Mordechai Anielewicz, who was only 23. This was probably Anielewicz. He bowed his head and said what he knew of the Kaddish prayer. When he finished he saw someone in the distance walking at the edge of the park. A man passing on the sidewalk had noticed him and from afar lifted his hat to him in a gesture of respect. He could then have asked the driver to take him to the Umschlagplatz, but he didn't. He didn't want to see it. The Umschlagplatz, the collection point in German, was the courtyard where the Germans forced the Jews to assemble before they led them to the trains. It wasn't necessary to see it, even though he'd been told that there was now a plaque there. Instead he told the driver to take him back to the hotel.

When they arrived the driver wanted to change money with him, and when he wouldn't change money, the driver was annoyed. Everyone in this country wanted to change zlotys for dollars. Soldiers, Boy Scouts, taxi drivers, the hotel maids. He just wanted to be left alone. He wasn't a money changer. He didn't acknowledge the doorman in the bearskin hat and gold-braided greatcoat, who solemnly held the cab door open. He ignored the doorman's assistance. He pushed into the lobby with its groups of tourists standing at the front desk and at the cashiers' cages. There were also some Polish officers and their wives, a few Russian officers in uniforms with red sideboards, and young Arab men reading and drinking coffee. He'd heard that the PLO trained guerillas in Czechoslovakia and that many of the Arab men in Warsaw were on leave from these camps. There was one fat older man in long robes who sat with them. He wore a fez, a monocle, and was reading a newspaper printed in Arabic.

He walked through the lobby and waited for the elevator to the casino bar. Up in the bar he ordered a brandy and drank it quickly. It burned as it went down and he ordered another and drank it just as quickly. Then he saw her getting up from a booth in the back of the room and walking toward him. She seemed to be covered with a green color, a soft, unusual, ancient green patina.

"Hello, American," she said. "Are you through with your communion?" She had eyes like a gray cat, and the tawny, sinister movements of a cat. "You see? I have waited for you. I knew you would be back. They all come back in about thirty minutes. Where are you from? Philadelphia? Boston?" She snapped her fingers at the bartender.

"Baltimore."

"Baltimore? I've never heard of it. Wladyslaw, I will have another Wyborowa, but over ice. How did you like the Ghetto? Did you go by Mercedes? There is nothing left to see there in the Ghetto. There is no Ghetto. Did you go to Mila Street?"

He signaled for another brandy. "No, I didn't know there was a Mila Street."

"Yes, of course, it was their headquarters there. Your countryman wrote a book, about it, what was his name...?"

"Leon Uris."

"Yes, Uris. Are you surprised I know of him? Of course I do. Jewish writers are very popular in Poland. Woody Allen. I know of him. We all love him. Even Jerzy Kosinski. He came back here only recently. It is a pity he committed suicide. Are you surprised that I know of American literature and films? Do you know I am a student at Warsaw University? Yes, a student of English literature. I come here occasionally, and if I see a man I like who will pay my price... I may go with him. Otherwise I just drink and read my book and go home alone. Did you ask me my price?" She shook her hair out at him. "My price is 1 million zlotys. What is it for you, a hundred dollars? Nothing. A meal or two. I can live on that for two months. And never have to come here. We will order a bottle of champagne and go to your room. Are you staying at the hotel?"

"I'm not interested in making love."

"Ah, love. Is that what you call it? I am not talking about love. We can discuss literature. What is your name?"

"Mark."

"Mark? That is not a Jewish name. That is the name of one of our saints, St. Mark. We have the name Marek."

"No, my name is Mark. What's your name?"

"My name? I never tell my name. Every time I have a different name. Tonight I shall also be a saint, St. Magdalena. Magda. She was also a whore. Our Lord Jesus was a Jew and he forgave her. Maria Magda. He blessed her as a saint and she washed his feet and dried them with her hair." She raised her glass. "Cheers, Marek. Drink your brandy."

He took the third brandy and now he was calm. The green that had colored her face was gone and he saw that she was dressed in black, almost like a young nun in her dark suit and immaculate white silk blouse. He remembered the young nuns as a child in Baltimore in the streets near his home, passing them on the sidewalk, their slim, high-planed faces, the ivory faces of the nuns as they passed murmuring in their black robes, the rustle of the hidden legs under the long robes.

"I'll go with you," he said. "Why not?"

"Good. We will buy a bottle of champagne and we will discuss literature." She snapped her fingers again at the barman. "Wladyslaw, champagne." She smiled at him for the first time. He reached out to her and with the same consciously gentle gesture touched her hair with the back of his hand, and then her face. This time she didn't turn away. He had always wanted to touch one of the ivory faces hidden behind the coifs and so now he determined he would do this and they would go together to his room.

"Before we leave, you must pay me my fee. Do you have dollars? I would prefer to be paid in dollars."

He had five $100 bills folded inside of a pocket in his checkbook. He removed the bills and handed her one. She looked at it quickly, opened it up and turned it over, and then opened her purse, put it in her wallet, and snapped her purse shut. She got off her stool. "Okay, let's go."

"I think I'll take another brandy to the room in a paper cup."

"How many brandies have you had?"

"Three or four."

"Wladyslaw, give the gentleman another brandy. Send it to his room. They won't allow you to take a paper cup through the lobby. Not even a glass. They're very decorous here. Did I say that right? I have difficulty with certain words."

"Yes, you said it right."

Up in the room, she put the bottle of champagne in the small refrigerator, removing most of the bottles of beer and wine the hotel had provided. He sat in a chair and watched as she moved around the room touching different articles. She went into the bathroom and came out with some plastic bottles of shampoo and lotion. "May I have these?"

"Yes."

She swept them into her purse. "And this?" She was holding a bar of milled French soap. She sniffed it and held it under his nose.

"Take it."

"Good. I can sell these things, you know, or keep them. I really don't need them. I prefer to sell them. How about this?" She held up a small sewing kit.

"Keep it."

"Thank you."

There was a knock on the door. "They're here already with your brandy."

He signed the check and gave the waiter a dollar. She

went back into the bathroom and opened the champagne. He heard the pop. She returned with a face towel around the bottle and poured two glasses. "There is a telephone in there !" she said. "That's really decadent. That's something new. In Poland people have nothing, and the guests here now have telephones in their bathrooms. How do you explain that?"

"That's capitalism."

"If that's capitalism, I don't want it."

"Well, you don't have to use the telephone."

She sat on the bed and raised her glass to him. "*Na zdrowie*, that's how we say cheers in Polish." She crossed her legs and then began swinging her leg. She leaned over to a panel at the side of the bed and turned down the lights. He reached out to her and in the half darkness traced the contours of her face with his index finger, and then her lips.

"Okay, we'll talk of literature," he said to her. "Do you know of the writer Isaac Bashevis Singer? He died yesterday in the States."

"No, I didn't know that. He was a very sweet man, Singer. He wrote the novel *Shosha*. Do you think I look like Shosha? I have her color of red hair."

He moved away from her and stood up and looked out the window. "I see Warsaw has a Coca Cola sign. It's the only sign I see."

"Yes, it's another gift from America. Coca Cola and a telephone in the bathroom. Just what we need." She shook up the bottle of champagne until it fizzed, and sprayed some of the champagne at the ceiling and then at him.

"You shouldn't do that."

"Why are you so quiet and sad, Marek? Is it because of Singer's death or your visit to the Ghetto, or are you drunk?"

He had difficulty focusing on her after four brandies. "I may be a little drunk."

"Are you a married man, Marek?"

"No, I was married."

"Where is your wife?"

"My wife? I have no wife."

She pushed another button for the radio at the night table. "Do you like Chopin? In Poland you can't escape him."

"Leave it on."

"Do you want to stay at the window? Why don't you sit on the bed?"

"Do you think Mary Magdalene really washed Christ's feet and dried them with her hair?"

"Is that what you want me to do for you? I won't do it."

"No, I don't want that."

"What do you want?"

"Do you know how to sew?"

"Sew? Yes, of course. Do you want me to give you the sewing kit back?"

"No, I want you to sew something for me. I don't know how to sew." He finished the brandy and sat down on the bed with her. "Did you take all the pens too?"

"Yes, pens and the letter sheets and envelopes. But I will give them back, and the sewing kit." She turned on the light and sat on the bed, and poured out the contents of her purse. Two plastic pens fell out with the sewing kit, several plastic bottles, the bar of soap, her wallet, a leather folio of stationery, and a letter opener and shears.

"You can have it all back, except for my wallet."

"No, you keep everything I just want to borrow a pen and the scissors from the stationery kit."

He began to draw a crude triangle on the yellow bedspread. He outlined a triangle, then bisected it with another triangle. He drew the design of the Star of David and then slowly lettered the word JUDE onto the center of the star. He took the scissors and cut the yellow star out of the bedspread. She watched him, sitting cross-legged, sipping champagne from the bottle. "You'll have to pay them," she finally said to him when he finished cutting out the star. "They won't allow this."

"I won't pay them. I don't care about their rules of decorum. I've already paid them."

"Now what?" She looked at him. She really was beautiful. Very inviting, very beautiful, with perfect Slavic eyes and cheekbones. She didn't look like Shosha though. He doubted if she was a student at the University. She was probably just a beautiful Polish hotel whore who liked to read. Although, maybe he was wrong, she could be a graduate student in literature. She knew too much about literature for her own good, and it disturbed him to have her as his seamstress. She was too intelligent. Now he just wanted her to leave. Maybe she was with the Polish version of the KGB, but what would they want from him? His book of photographs of the Warsaw Ghetto that he bought yesterday? *Getto Warszawskie*? Photos of Jews begging, skeletal children, hollow-eyed, dying in the streets?

He went to the closet and got his navy blue blazer and put it down in front of her on the bed. "Can you sew this star on my jacket? Right there?" He pointed to the breast pocket.

"Sew it?"

"Yes, right there. Sew this and you can go. You'll make Poland's last Jew. While you're doing that, I think I'll go into the bathroom and phone God and tell him what I'm doing. Use good strong basting stitches."

He went to the bathroom and ran water over his fingers

and touched his face, and looked at himself in the mirror. She was right, he did look like a Jew. He spread his fingers in a fan in front of the mirror. He did have dark fingers.

"You're sewing?"

"Yes, be quiet. I haven't done this in a long time. You are a bit crazy, you know."

"And so are you."

"Yes, we are a good pair, a Catholic whore, Maria Magdalena, and a Jewish saint, St. Marek from Baltimore."

"I don't know who you are, but I'm not a Jewish saint."

"Did you telephone to God?"

"Yes, I did."

"What did you ask him"?"

"I asked him why three million Jews died here."

"And what did he say?"

"He said he didn't know."

"Do you accept that answer?"

"No."

"There." She held the jacket out and showed it to him with the star sewn on the breast pocket. "It's done."

"You're sure that it will hold? The stitches are strong?"

"Yes, of course. My grandmother taught me that cross-stitch. I call it Basia's stitch. It is done. It will last."

"Thank you very much. You may go now. Take the sewing kit, take the pens, all the bottles. Take everything."

She swept all the articles back into her purse. "You will be all right, Marek? Where will you go with that star on your jacket?" She looked at herself in the mirror and patted her hair. He could see that she had finished with him. She wasn't really interested in him, and in a minute would disappear forever.

"I don't know where I'll go."

She took a bottle of cologne from her purse and

sprayed her wrists and throat. "I will leave you now, Marek, okay?"

"Yes, and take the bottle of champagne."

"I cannot believe you have given me a million zlotys for sewing, Marek. Only from an American. Someday, when I come to America, I will look you up." She opened the door, put her purse over her shoulder, and carried her shoes in her hand. She looked at him. "Ciao," she said, and instead of taking the elevator, she was suddenly gone, down the stairway.

He put the jacket on. She'd done a good job. He touched the star on his pocket and smoothed the hair at his temples, and caught the empty elevator downstairs. No one was in the lobby, no one paid attention to him as he passed. One man in front of the hotel stared at him and then quickly turned away.

He walked over to the plaza where the two young guards were still marching in cadence, and watched them. There were torches burning and a small crowd. No one noticed him, and he watched for a few moments and then moved to a park bench and sat down in the shadows of the trees.

If he'd had a portable phone with him, he could have called God again, but he wasn't in America so he didn't have a portable phone. If he'd had one, he could have set it on redial. He didn't have one, though, and he folded his arms around himself and sat quietly at the rim of the torchlight. He looked at his fingers. He did have dark fingers, even in the torchlight.

Suddenly she came up to him out of the shadows.

"Why are you sitting here, Marek? I saw you leaving the hotel."

He didn't answer her.

"You know, it won't do any good for you to sit here with your star, Marek."

She reached out to him and touched his cheek with almost

the same gesture he'd used. "I'm going for my tram now. You really shouldn't stay here. Someone may hurt you. Do you understand that? You should go back to your hotel."

He watched her turn and slowly walk away from him towards the plaza. She turned back once more and called out to him, "You shouldn't stay there, Marek. It is dangerous for you to sit there." She stood looking at him for a moment and then shrugged and walked toward the shadows of the torchlight and she was gone.

Lederhosen
Boys

L · B · K

WHEN I WAS A BOY, growing up as a young Jew in Milwaukee, in 1937 when I was about ten, an immigrant German family moved into a house on our block. I remember them as tall, blonde people with two little boys named Abner and Henning who, when they first came to our block, used to play dressed in lederhosen outfits in front of their house. They were ruddy-faced, blue-eyed blondes like their parents and, of course, when they first arrived, they stayed mostly to themselves, occasionally venturing as far as the parkway to poke out with sticks at stones lying in the street gutter. My mother had taught me to ask their names in German, *"Was ist ihr name?"* and one day I approached them and tried the phrase out. *"Was ist ihr name?"* I said to one of them who was crouched in his lederhosen poking stones into the sewer grating at the curb. "Abner," he said, and his brother replied, "Henning." Not understanding that they were answering me, I repeated the question again and again and each time they responded,

"Abner, Henning," until finally all three of us were red faced and shouting. Then, as I remember, the little boys looked up at me disgustedly and ran back up on their porch into their house and slammed the door. My only memory of Abner and Henning other than this shouting match is later when I traded them my skeleton ring for a blue covered paper booklet, about the size and appearance of a literary quarterly. The booklet was a document of crimes allegedly committed by the Czechs against the Sudeten-land Germans. It was printed in English and contained lurid tales of rapes of Sudeten maidens by Czech constabulary, spelled out in sufficient detail to warrant a special hiding place in my closet. To this date, I still wonder about the significance of that booklet in the little German boys' background.

Were they really refugees from Hitler or was their father sent to Milwaukee for liaison with the German American Bund? I do not know.

But then, as I reached back in memory, and it is difficult because almost thirty-five years have passed, I do remember one other meeting with the little German boys. In my infancy, I was cared for by a series of nursemaids and one of them had taught me a child's phrase in German, *Der hund läuft der katze nach.* The dog runs after the cat. One day, it must have been during the same summer—I do remember it was after my miserable attempts with *Was ist ihr name?*—I again encountered Abner and Henning on their front sidewalk. This time, and without coaching from my mother, I tried my own phrase on them. The two lederhosen boys were bent over at the curb again at the matter of poking stones. They turned on their haunches and squinted up at me. "Good morning," I said in English, and then followed with *Der hund läuft der katze nach.* They both immediately stood and gazed far up and down the street and then back at me again. I nodded. They nodded rather mistrustingly, I now suppose. Then

I repeated my nurse's sentence, *Der hund läuft der katze nach.* Again the two boys looked up and down the street and then at me. *Der hund läuft der katze nach.* I said again and then again. This time they didn't bother to run into the house. They simply turned their backs to me and resumed poking their stones. After this encounter, we never again spoke, except perhaps for the matter of trading the ring for the Sudeten crimes booklet. In any event, I have no further memory of Abner and Henning.

I don't know why these memories should come back to touch upon me some thirty-five years later. I am now a lawyer in Chicago, with a family, living the suburban life, commuting to an office in the city. Yet the two little lederhosen boys suddenly arise fresh in my memory. Perhaps they come so freshly to me now because of certain photographs that I found in an old *Life* magazine the other afternoon.

About three weeks ago, on a Sunday afternoon, I drove my wife and children to Chicago to visit some friends who live in a walk-up apartment and have children who are playmates of our children. We spent the afternoon on the back porch while the children played in the courtyard, several floors below us. About mid-afternoon, the adults went shopping at a neighborhood grocery for our dinner and I was left alone on the porch with a freshened drink and some old *Life* magazines from the forties that our friends thought would be interesting. The first issue I picked up featured a photo-essay on a concentration camp that had been liberated by the American Army as it fought its way into Germany. There was a photograph of a group of Jewish prisoners dressed in striped convict uniforms, each wearing a square hat, all standing behind barbed wire. The photograph must have been taken as the GIs approached the front gate of the camp, because the prisoners appeared to be standing in an attitude of formality that I now regard as that of welcoming their liberators, although

181

the prisoners' faces showed no expression. It was almost as if the photograph had been taken through a heavy rain and behind the rain were forms, human in shape, but coming into the lens only as shadows. There were several other photographs of the concentration camp. One was of the electric fence around the camp that was separated by a moat. Just at the edge of the moat, the Germans had screened the fence with grass and birch trees. It had the appearance of a median strip on a new highway, immaculately attended, everything orderly, the young birch saplings guyed down with wires and their fragile trunks wrapped with protective coverings. There was also a photograph of an oven and piles of human bones and skulls.

The shock of seeing these photographs in the old magazine brought memories to me of other pictures hidden deep in my consciousness. I suppose we all have these films stored within us, reminding us of tragedies, old loves, triumphs, all the categories of memory. Mine are racked up in neat files, almost, I suppose, in gray tin movie spools, stacked like they are in a projectionist's booth, with worn bits of adhesive tape on each spool identifying the subject matter. Sometimes, when I run my films, the actors, including myself, come vividly to the screen as they were in life at that time. Other times, the forms are murky, my memory having to pump and creak to keep the film going, infusing color and comment into the central events. I'm sure that I've engaged in quite a bit of re-casting and having the prerogative of both producer and director, I've altered the dialogue and events to favor myself.

But some of the films I carry within me, unedited, particularly the one of Jewish suffering, because these are films in which I had no personal participation and were merely recorded by me as an adolescent mostly from magazine pictures and newsreels. Usually these films, stripped of nostalgia and personality, were recorded by me for private reasons, probably to fulfill certain emotional needs. In the case of the film of the suffering of the Jews in World War II, the emotion it brings immediately is hatred. Not necessarily hatred of the War and all human suffering, but pure, absolute hatred of the Germans.

Now, the old photographs in the *Life* magazine immediately triggered my own films and I show them to you now, a series of photographs accumulated by me as a young American Jew and strung together in this manner.

Frame One

A blurred photo of Jewish merchants on their knees, old men dressed in formal black suits and derby hats. They are sweeping the sidewalks in front of their shops of broken glass. In the photograph a group of smiling young men in brownshirt uniforms and swastika armbands wave their clubs in mock salute to the photographer.

Frame Two

Jewish prisoners being led away under gunpoint from the Warsaw Ghetto. A column of about thirty people, marching in rows of four or five abreast, one German soldier at the front of the column. This German carries a rifle, or perhaps a machine pistol, the stock in his right armpit, the barrel pointed to the ground. He too is smiling for the photographer. In the background the ghetto buildings burn in clouds of black smoke. The Jews each carry a suitcase or a bundle of personal belongings. In the first row of the column, facing the cameraman, there appears one family, a grandmother, father and mother, and a child, a little girl of about four. They are dressed as middle-class people, the man in a tie, suit and vest, his wife in a cloth coat with a fur collar.

The child with one hand holds the edge of her mother's coat and in the other carries a doll. The people all have their faces averted from the camera; only the child, in perfect innocence, stares directly at the photographer.

Frame Three

A stack of bodies piled on the back of a cart or a truck, the corpses so stiff they seem frozen, hands dangle, mouths gape with unanswered screams.

Frame Four

The station platform at Auschwitz. A photograph probably taken from a rooftop, the camera looking down through the haze of engine smoke on prisoners assembled alongside a freight train. German soldiers with whips and dogs keep the columns in order.

Frame Five

Jews somewhere in Poland being forced to dig their graves while German guards, rifles in hand, stand above them on a dirt abutment. The prisoners dig with long-handled spades, most of the men elderly and bearded and dressed in black caftans.

Frame Six

Piles of hair shorn from the bodies of gassed victims. Another pile of gold teeth heaped neatly together.

Frame Seven

A group of Jewish prisoners in tiered bunks in a concentration camp barracks. The photo seemingly taken at the moment the barracks door was forced open. There, in the light coming through the door, prisoners lie staring at the first intrusion of light. All are too weak for movement or gesture.

Frame Eight

Two children, a boy of about six, a girl of perhaps four, alone at some prisoner collection point, maybe a railroad siding. Each is dressed in a dark overcoat, the boy with a peaked cap, the little girl in a beret. They are certainly brother and sister. The boy has his arm around his sister. Each has at his side a suitcase. Each has pinned to his breast a Star of David emblem. The little girl has black curls and a baby face still softly rounded between infancy and adolescence. The boy has dark hair but his features are sharper and gaunt. No childhood gaiety lingers about them. Both gravely face the cameraman, certain of their abandonment, two lost children on their way to death, yet still together as brother and sister.

End of Film

Why did I run these films for you now? I do not know. I do know that once they have begun they must be shown through to conclusion and the process of viewing them, each time, leaves me drained. I suppose it is a form of expiation. It works to some extent, although my hatred of the Germans is by now such a basic part of me that **it** cannot be washed away by the showing of a few old films. Perhaps the only function the film showing serves is that it helps unreel the layers of my memory and ultimately takes me back to my childhood in Milwaukee so that the two lederhosen boys appear fresh and vivid through the grayness and agony of all the old films.

Even by running the films to clear the memory, I have difficulty remembering those days in Milwaukee. Of course, I have the other films of childhood, and these I could run to assist me, but I choose not to, because the film that I have run brings me to a certain focus that I do not want to abandon.

As a ten-year-old in Milwaukee in 1937 my vision, of

course, was that of a young American schoolboy, My family was not a religious family, although both my parents had formal religious training and strong Jewish identification. But our Jewishness was more of an allegiance than a discipline. We thought of ourselves as Americans, not as Jews, except in some kind of unspoken cultural obeisance. I was busy as a bugler boy in the American Legion post marching band. My father played night softball as a graceful, dark-haired shortstop on a businessmen's team of mostly gentile players. My parents' circle of friends was made up of Jews, a dentist, some merchants, a lawyer. But my parents were also friendly with the neighbors on the block, although we were the only Jewish family. In the evenings, occasionally my mother and father would sit with these gentile neighbors on their porches and drink lemonade, although now I realize that none of them ever came to the house as guests and my parents never went to their homes. Still, my father would laugh and joke with these neighborhood men as I played softball catch with him in front of our house or as he stood in the evening and watered our lawn. In the neighborhood, he was the same graceful Jewish shortstop, darting here and there to touch upon and join the life of the neighborhood and then withdrawing. I suppose he was always essentially alien in their eyes, but despite being a Jew, he was viewed as a rather nice man who almost every evening threw grounders to his son on the front walk until the street lights blinked on. But as a child, I was not aware of our separateness. My friends were the gentile boys from the block. We were schoolmates together. Although our parents observed an acquiesced separateness, we were unaware of it. Far past the streetlight hour, we played our games into the night, Red Rover, Washington Post, Hide and Seek, until one by one our fathers came out to whistle for us with that particular whistling call that I still remember and identify with those soft Milwaukee nights of my childhood.

I do not remember any overt acts of anti-Semitism among my friends or their parents. But now with the running of my film and having focused in on my life as a young Jew in Milwaukee, one afternoon in particular is evoked. Essentially the film device is selective and evocative and re-creates certain events with a clarity that justifies the pain of seeing all these old pictures. One Sunday afternoon comes into focus. My parents and I enjoyed driving to Port Washington, a little town near Milwaukee, about fifteen miles outside the city. Port Washington was really just a lake town. Like many towns that border Lake Michigan, it had some industry, but there were boats there and fishermen and a small fishing fleet. On Sundays we liked to walk out on the piers and look at the boats. Afterwards, we would stop at Smith Brothers restaurant where they served fresh fish sandwiches. But on this Sunday, I remember there was very heavy traffic on the road to Port Washington. The people seemed to be headed for an outing or picnic and the cars we passed were full of children. Then, as we came toward an iron railroad bridge, we could see that someone had painted a message in large white letters on the side of the bridge. As we approached the bridge we could see the message, spelled in whitewash, "Kill the Jews, Buy Gentile." As we came under the bridge there was a small hill and when we reached the top of the hill we could see thousands of people in the distance out in a field. The men were dressed in the brown-shirted uniform of the German American Bund and they were having a picnic and soccer games. There were literally thousands of people in that field, almost an army of men in brown shirts and military britches, the brown color of their uniforms seemed to cover the earth out to the horizon. At the edge of the highway there was a flagpole, and on the flagpole the German swastika flag was flying.

So now having run my film and having been brought

back to my memories of those Milwaukee days, I somewhat understand what it would have been like for a Jewish boy growing up in Munich in the early thirties. The question is always asked, why did the Jews stay in Germany? Of course, some did get out, but most like that young American Jew in Milwaukee whose father played shortstop on the businessmen's team, remained. The families were confident of their assimilation. They thought as Germans, not as Jews. If the Nazis were forming their divisions, it was on some distant hillside on a pleasant Sunday afternoon. Of course, this is all known, and nothing new is brought to light by these statements. But these films are my own, and I choose to run them, on occasion, in any event.

My wife and I still return with our children now and then to Milwaukee. It is only an hour from our Chicago suburb and a pleasant drive. Today, it is a huge industrial city with great factories and expressways. One evening this summer, we drove to Milwaukee and as we drove through the near west side of the city we saw a church carnival with rides and a Ferris wheel. Our children were excited so we parked the car and went to the carnival. The neighborhood people were there with their children, mostly bright-eyed little Poles and Germans, skipping around long rows of picnic tables that had been set up in a circle around a small wooden dance floor. People were drinking pitchers of beer and eating bratwurst sandwiches. An old man, full of energy, played the concertina and whistled polka shrills to the couples dancing and stomping.

It was another of those soft Milwaukee evenings and I took my daughter up on the Ferris wheel. When we came to the top, we were held there for our turn and I could look out over the lights of the city. The big, square lighted clock from the Allen-Bradley factory faced me, perhaps one of the largest clocks in the world, it stands over the city as a symbol of discipline and order. All seemed in order. I remembered a professor at the University of Michigan, Austin Warren, who had written a collection of criticism titled, *A Rage for Order,* taken from a line of Wallace Stevens' poem, "The Idea of Order at Key West." Perhaps that is it after all, the essential madness of man, A Rage for Order. As we rocked on the Ferris wheel I stared back at the huge, lighted clock. But I could feel the old films coming again, and I was glad that our turn would soon be over and we would begin our descent back to the ground before the lederhosen boys would come poking with their sticks to haunt me with more evocations. For the process of film showing is evocative and the Milwaukee night, even as you begin your descent on a Ferris wheel, already lies softly on your cheek. I have also seen Key West and there, I must report, the same soft night wind blows against those who ride Ferris wheels down.

Messenger

L·B·K

I WENT TO HIGH SCHOOL in a northern suburb of Chicago. I began in 1941 and was graduated in 1945. So I missed World War II, but during my high school years classmates were constantly going off to war. Many of them returned wounded, and quite a few never returned. The town maintained a large white billboard in a parking lot behind one of the clothing stores on Main Street. All the boys who were in the service had their names printed in blue letters on the billboard with their rank and branch of service. Those who died in the war had their names lettered in gold. The same system was used to indicate a family that lost a son. If a son was in the service, a small fringed silk banner would hang in a front window. The banner was edged in red with a white field and a blue star in the center. If a son had died, the star in the center would be gold. Since our town was then quite small, we knew the houses where the gold star banners hung. Even in my early years of high school I knew most of the boys who had been killed.

Late in 1944 classmates began to come home on leave after being wounded. We would suddenly encounter them between classes, gray faced, hollow cheeked, sitting on the steps of the auditorium in their wrinkled uniforms. They never spoke about the war. They'd nod hello shyly and suck deeply on their cigarettes. I remember one boy who had returned with chest wounds from Iwo Jima. I encountered him one afternoon in the winter of 1944 after school at the pool hall. I hadn't seen him since he enlisted. We'd been good friends and he was a halfback on our football team. He was a year older than most of us and he had left school in his junior year and enlisted in the Marine Corps. His face now was gaunt and very pale. You could see that he had been through a great ordeal and all his youthful gaiety had distilled into a kind of sad wisdom. When I saw him at the pool hall his Marine gloves were folded through one of the epaulets on his shoulder. He was squinting and trying to use a bridge to get a line on a shot. He wore the single red bordered chevron of a PFC and Good Conduct and Purple Heart ribbons. He was in great pain but he tried to shoot pool with me for a while. After the game I helped him on with his Marine greatcoat and he walked back out into the snowstorm. I've never seen him again.

I still live in the same town. I commute to my office as a lawyer in Chicago thirty miles on a commuter train. I mention this only because I want you to know the perspective I have is that of a man of fifty with the particular biases and inclinations of that age. When I move about the town now, I am often haunted by the memory of the young boys I knew who died in the war. Sometimes I still fill with bitterness. At the supermarket in summer I see women in tennis dresses shopping leisurely with sunglasses back in their hair. As I watch them ordering the young grocery boys around, the sad pale faces of some of my dead friends come back to me. I know this is irrational but perhaps there is a connecting point. Our town was divided by class. There were many wealthy old families and the mothers and daughters of those families in summertime often wore tennis dresses while they shopped, having just rushed into the store from the country clubs before dinner. I was a guest of my classmates at these country clubs during the summer. I can remember the tanned, fresh faces of the women in their tennis dresses standing proudly with a son or brother in uniform for a photograph at poolside or at a tennis court. I don't know why I should still be filled with resentment. What should the women have done? Should they have fought the Germans and Japanese? I don't know. Maybe some of the women should have also fought and been maimed and killed. I do know that today when I see the young women shoppers in their white tennis dresses instructing the grocery boys, I fill with these irrational tracings of anger.

During the War, we were put through a physical training course at the high school. Every day we'd change into shorts or a sweat suit and run an obstacle course that had been quickly built into a ravine behind our auditorium. There were long ropes hung over a ditch and various walls and barriers erected in the gullies of the ravine. You would run down a hill at top speed, grab the rope and swing yourself over the ditch. We'd yell "Geronimo" as we swung over the ditch, or "Air Force," or "Navy," depending on the particular service we were going to join. Each day after running the obstacle course we'd come up out of the ravine and form squads and run through the streets of the town for the balance of the hour. The gym instructors ran at our sides in sweat suits, white towels wrapped around their throats. They'd lead us, "Hut two. ..hut two.. ." gray sweatsuited lines tramping down the snow-covered streets. Our instructor was a square jawed man; he'd run backwards and watch us for a few steps, his breath pluming in the icy air..."Square it up, square it up..." Then we'd sing the Marine Hymn at the top of our lungs and stamp our feet in cadence.

During my junior year I took an after school job working for Western Union. The Western Union office was in a storefront across from the railroad station. There was a high varnished counter as you entered. A rack of printed samples of telegrams was placed on the counter so a customer could select form birthday or anniversary messages. There were several large metal tables for supplies. Mildred Everson was the manager of the office and she sat in the rear in front of the Teletype machine sending messages or stripping messages which she had received. Miss Everson never told me about the messages that were preceded by four stars, " * * * * Mrs. Jane Doe, 1234 Main Street." At least I think she hadn't told me about the four-star telegrams. I must have been fifteen or sixteen when I took the job.

She gave me the first four-star telegram about a week after I began work. I got on my bicycle and rode to the address. It was addressed to a woman who lived in a second floor walkup apartment across the tracks. I parked my bike and walked up the stairs, down a long corridor, and knocked on the apartment door. I heard a young woman's voice. She opened the door, a short blonde woman of about 22. I still remember her shy smile as I handed her the envelope. She went into another room and came back with a quarter. She smiled at me again, her eyes still remain in my memory, trusting and innocent. As I reached the stairway and started back down I heard the first shriek. I walked slowly down the stairway and I could hear her screaming. I gently closed the front door and jumped on my bike and rode back to the office. I believe I then asked Miss Everson what was in the telegram and she told me. The young woman had been notified that her brother had been killed in Germany. I still don't know if I'm

196

telling myself the truth. It was my first job, and faced with the choice of delivering the message of death or losing the job, I could have lacked the resolution to refuse. In any event, I was the boy who delivered that message and the wild shrieking of the woman in the dark hallway still accuses me.

I could have then chosen to resign but I stayed on. I think I had convinced myself that because of my sensitivity I should become the death messenger for the town. I would console each person and comfort them. I had grown up in the community. The young men being killed were my classmates. Someone had to deliver the messages. If not me, some stranger with less insight would be the messenger. I remained on.

The machine sounded a bell four times when each four star message was received. "Ding, ding, ding, ding." Miss Everson and I would rush to the machine and watch it as it began to type out the name. She was a tall, slim woman, her hair in tight pin curls, thin lipped, with steel rimmed glasses. She always wore a rubber thimble on her right hand and was stoop shouldered from so many years of sitting at the machine. Maybe she was just a taciturn Swedish spinster, but her hands as she stripped the tapes from the machine, measuring and cutting them into lines, were slim, ivory, beautiful hands. Her fingernails were long and painted bright red. It was the one touch of adornment, her only cosmetic. It always was startling to see her plain face with the steel rimmed glasses and then her beautiful ivory hands with the red nails working the keys of the machine. But even though I thought I could do the job, as the death messages came and became more frequent, I refused to deliver them. Miss Everson would put on her old fur coat and call a taxi and deliver them herself. When she returned she'd be very quiet and we wouldn't discuss my refusal. I don't know why she didn't fire me. I think she just wanted someone to keep her company.

I did take one more message. Miss Everson was ill with the flu and the town was paralyzed by a winter storm. There were only two taxis and they were both out of service. The message was for a family at the north end of town, a section where mostly working class Italian families lived. I had known many of these boys from the football and baseball teams. Also, some of the Italian boys hung around the pool hall. The dead boy's name was Luigi Modico. I knew Luigi Modico but not well. I played baseball with him. He was a shortstop with a good arm, a senior when I was a freshman. I remember how he used to exhort his teammates in Italian, "*Andiamo, andiamo!*" [let's go] Then he'd spit and whistle with an unusually shrill sound like a screech owl. I remembered Luigi as a shortstop, not as a soldier. The telegram was addressed to Mr. and Mrs. Albert Modico. It had the requisite four stars.

* * * * THE SECRETARY OF WAR REGRETS TO INFORM YOU OF THE DEATH OF YOUR SON PRIVATE LUIGI MODICO, UNITED STATES ARMY, WHO DIED IN THE DEFENSE OF HIS COUNTRY IN GERMANY ON JANUARY 4, 1945. IT IS WITH THE DEEPEST REGRET THAT WE ADVISE YOU OF HIS DEATH. FURTHER DETAILS WILL FOLLOW. WITH SYMPATHY. HENRY L. STIMSON. SECRETARY OF WAR. BY THE ADJUTANT GENERAL.

I took my bicycle out to the icy streets. It must have taken an hour of alternately riding and walking the bike because the streets were so rutted with ice before I reached the Modico house. It was a small white frame clapboard cottage on a wooded lot. I could see the lights of a Christmas tree through the windows and some people in the living room. I stacked the bike outside the gate and walked up the path. An older man answered the door, Luigi's father, short and dark faced, with Luigi's thick legs. He invited me in. I could see a fire crackling. There was a serviceman's banner hung in the window, a single blue-fringed silk star. I tried to explain that I had a telegram but Mr. Modico did not understand. A young man in a Marine uniform came to the door. I recognized him from the pool hall. His name was Carlo Ruffolatti. We called him "Ruffo." He must have been home on leave after basic training. I knew he was a good friend of Luigi's. Ruffo was a tiny kid, he had the build of a jockey and he was sparrow faced. Now I realize his face could have been taken from a Venetian frieze, the face of a doge or a wizened emissary. He nodded hello at me. His Marine uniform was ill fitting and his hair was shorn to his scalp. He wore the new silver badge of a Marine sharpshooter.

"Hello, Ruffo," I said to him. "I have a telegram for Luigi's family." I held the envelope up. He looked at me suspiciously. He'd been drinking with the family. A wine bottle was on the table near the fireplace. He looked at me and stared. I saw the father watching me. The mother came in from the kitchen, wiping her hands on her apron. She smiled at me. I handed Ruffo the telegram and went out the door. "Ruffo, you tell them," I said. "Please tell them."

I slowly began to walk my bike. It was snowing again very heavily and the wind blew snow in my face. I got up on the bike and tried to ride in the ruts. After riding two blocks I stood and rested under a street lamp and made a mask for my face with my muffler. I went another twenty feet when suddenly someone pushed me from behind and threw me down. I fell in the snow and rolled. Ruffo was standing there. "What do you think I am," he said. "You think I should tell them Luigi is dead?" I could see he hadn't even bothered to put his coat on, he was wearing a white silk scarf and his leather Marine gloves. "Ruffo, someone has to tell them." "Shut up," he said. I saw him reach down inside his Marine jacket. "No one has to tell them." He pulled out a Colt .45. The gun was huge. He held it with both hands. I could hear the hammer click. "No more words," he said to me. He pushed me in the back with the gun. "Walk." We marched through the ice storm, block after block in silence, until finally we were at the high school, the ravine where the obstacle course was built. He prodded me up on the hill and said, "Now you're gonna run the course and when you get down there," he was pointing to the rope over the gully, "you gonna grab that rope and swing." He pointed again with the gun and began to count. "One, two, three, run." I didn't move. "Run!" I began sliding down the hill and grabbed at the rope. It was coated with ice. I slipped and fell into the gully. I could see Ruffo standing at the top of the ravine. He was still holding the gun with both hands and aiming at me. I rolled away from him, crashing through the ice in the gully, tearing with my hands at the bare trees. I dove behind the obstacle course wall. I got down at the base of the wall. I could hear him walking down the side of the ravine, the ice crackling as he came toward me. I waited. I didn't think he could see me. I pulled myself up again and he was standing there. He had the gun aimed at me. "The gun is empty," he finally said to me and pointed it down. He spit on the ground and handed me the telegram. It was unopened.

I watched him leave. He turned and walked away, crunching up the hill until he got to the top. "Stay out of our part of town," he yelled to me. "*Basta*," he yelled. I knew what it meant. I'd heard it often at school, *Basta*. [enough] Then he pointed the gun up and fired once into the air.

I did quit the job as Western Union boy that night. I never told Miss Everson or anyone why I quit. I just walked back to the office and gave her Luigi Modico's telegram. The next day I went back for my bicycle. I never called her again. I suppose she delivered it in the morning. In any event, a few days later Luigi Modico had his name lettered in gold on the billboard. The day after I quit the messenger job there was a sign in the window, "Wanted - After School - Messenger Boy -See Manager Inside."

Ruffo survived the war and I see him occasionally at the station. He's a construction foreman and works for a contractor in Chicago. Usually, he's met at the train by his wife, a slim woman who drives a white Chevy van. Ruffo is now gray-haired and wears a pair of horn-rimmed glasses as he reads the paper. He lost his left arm in the war. He does not wear a prosthetic device. His sleeve is neatly tucked and pinned. He is always pleasant. We've never spoken about the incident with the gun or about the war. When I see him riding into the city reading the *Tribune*. I look at him and remember the way he was at eighteen in his Marine uniform. But then as I stare at him across the aisle, the faces of the young boys I knew who died in the war begin to come back. I close my eyes and try to shut out the pale, young, dead faces, but they insist on coming, one by one, and now they're always preceded by the warning signal of the teletype machine as the slender keys begin tapping out the names. Sometimes the faces are so vivid that I want to reach out and touch them or shake them as they pass. So far, I have avoided doing that.

Lowell B. Komie has written four collections of short stories, *The Judge's Chambers, The Lawyer's Chambers and Other Stories,* which won the Carl Sandburg Award for Fiction, *The Night Swimmer: A Man in London and Other Stories,* and his most recent, *The Legal Fiction of Lowell B. Komie.* He is the author of three novels, *The Last Jewish Shortstop in America,* winner of the Small Press Award for Fiction, *Conversations with a Golden Ballerina,* and *The Humpback of Lodz.*

Printed in the United States
58772LVS00005B/91-99

9 780964 195769